ALL MEN LOVE LEAH

A Novel

By Ksenija Nikolova

KINGSLEY
PUBLISHERS

Dedication

I dedicate this book to all the wallflowers out there, trying their best and silently battling mental health problems. You are not alone. Life will be beautiful again. You can do this.

Chapter 1

It's August and it's unbearably hot in Pisa, tourists pass by and take photographs, enjoying themselves. Everyone seems happy, maybe they are happy, or maybe they just act like they are. Nothing is clear to me. I see the sun beat down on them. I see beads of sweat form on their brows. I feel sorry for them because they must be so uncomfortable in the heat. No; I don't feel sorry for them. It's their fault. They know how hot it is, yet they go out, then they complain about the sun. I don't understand people.

I stand at my apartment window smoking a cigarette and look at the emptiness in front of me. It feels like I'm so close to the people passing by, I can almost touch them. They normally go to the Square with the crooked tower. It's the main attraction for tourists but it means nothing to me. It's just proof that in this world something has to happen all the time for something else to happen. I stand and enjoy my cigarette. I don't want to rush, even though my parents will come back from lunch anytime now. My parents don't know that I smoke. I am twenty-nine years old, and my parents still don't know that I smoke. Their opinion means everything to me. Maybe that is pathetic, but that is how it is. It works well like that to be honest. It's convenient. I get to enjoy my daily habits and they don't know I'm doing anything they don't approve of. I simply do as I please. I always do as I please.

I am obsessed with the thought that everything is absolutely in vain, and that every human being is born the way he is meant to be, and it cannot be escaped.

The tourists are very loud. They are very, very loud. I have a feeling that in their country they are not the same people. I have a feeling that they are waiting to travel somewhere to show their true selves, to laugh out loud, to shout and run in the streets. Maybe it's illogical to think that - I don't know, but I suspect it's true. Where does that joy; that serenity; that energy come from? Are these people ever sad; or are they programmed so that when they travel, they are constantly happy? I don't know. On the other hand, maybe the trip itself makes them happy, and in those moments, there is joy. I don't want to travel. It's too complicated for me. I've never been anywhere. I don't want to go anywhere; even the thought of it tires me. Don't all the cities look like each other? You can't see anything new. You just imagine that something is different, but in fact the same image, the same story is constantly repeating itself - expensive restaurants, loud tourists, long queues, and incredible congestion. It's all nonsense. I avoid it. I decide that travel is overrated.

One more drag of my cigarette and I'm finished smoking. Maybe I will have time for another smoke. Yes, I will definitely have time for another. I will light one more, and if I hear my parents coming in, I will run to the toilet. I feel good when I light a new cigarette. I wish I could smoke it in silence, but that is impossible here in the summer because there are tourists everywhere.

I look out the window and see a child with an ice cream, all dirty and running. The ice-cream is dripping but no one says anything. Is that joy? I don't understand. I look out at a woman in high heels. She can barely walk. Her feet must be sore. She must be very tired. I wonder why she does that to herself. Why she does not stay home, or put on comfortable shoes?

The woman appears at the window in front of me. She's wearing a grey coat and has long, dark brown hair. Her hair falls, hiding her face. I focus my attention on her. She runs and her coat flows behind her. It strikes me as odd. She stops to tie her coat and looks around as if she is looking for something.

She catches my gaze from where I'm standing at the window. We look into each other's eyes and she smiles, but she keeps running. After a few seconds, I lose sight of her. Her face is like a little girl's. Her stature is proud and strong, but perfect. I feel like I have seen her somewhere, I feel like I know her. I must have seen her somewhere before, but if I had, I would have remembered. I would certainly have remembered her. A woman like her is not easily forgotten, that's for sure. I consider that it's because I like her, so I feel like I know her, but I don't really know her at all. I only know I like the way I feel when I look at her. I can't make sense of how I feel, but I look at her until I can't see her anymore.

Later, she is an image stuck in my head. I can't stop thinking about her – the mysterious woman who wears a coat when it is hot outside. I hear my parents come in. I hide my cigarette, run to the bathroom, and shut the door. I pretend to take a shower, but I'm not even thinking about what I'm doing. The woman in the grey coat is the only thing on my mind.

.   .   .

The next morning I wake up with the usual desire for the day to be identical to the previous day. It's quite common for me to feel like this. I enjoy living that way. There is nothing more beautiful than habits, consistency, avoiding any risk, ignoring the unknown. People deliberately choose the opposite and then complain that they have new problems. I'm happy I'm not like them.

The image of the woman from yesterday pops into my head again. I don't understand myself. Why is she in my head again? It doesn't make sense. It's hard to survive in my head. I know that, that's why I wonder.

I want to push time to pass by a little faster. I have always thought that time passes too slowly, and I wish someone would do something about it. I can't understand people who complain that they don't have time for anything, and that time passes too quickly. I have time for everything, and in the end I still have so much time left that I don't know what to do with myself.

My parents are going out again but I decided to stay home. My home is the most beautiful place. I watch TV, I think, I eat whatever I want, and whenever I am alone - I smoke cigarettes.

I start watching a movie, knowing in advance that the movie does not deserve my attention. There is a boring movie on TV. Every boring movie on TV is a reason for a new cigarette. I stand at the window, light one, and feel wonderful.

There are so many tourists again, running and taking pictures. They are chasing the new, hot day in Pisa; thinking they can seize it; thinking chasing the day is seizing it. I think they are fools, amazing fools, all of them! Where are they running? Why are they in a hurry?! Do they think they can change things? Do they think they can achieve anything? People are so average. People complain that they never have time because they unknowingly chase time away from themselves. Time runs away from them because they are constantly trying to hold onto it. They squeeze it with both hands, they squeeze as much fresh juice out of it as possible, and then they drink the juice, expecting a miracle to happen. It can't be done that way. It can't work that way. Everything has been decided already. Everything has been thought out a long time ago. People will never be more powerful than time. I truly pity them for being creatures full of hope.

"Hey, where are you going?" It sounds like a voice shouting at me as I close the window. It seems like the voice was addressing me. There are so many people passing by my window, I can't see who it was that spoke.

I lie down on the couch in the living room and stretch out my body. I stare at the TV. I try to make myself comfortable. Nothing happens. Nothing happens in this movie.

I try to ignore the fact that what I'm watching has no point, but I can't ignore it. My mom always tells me that absolutely all movies have a point. Maybe it's my fault. Maybe I just don't understand the movie. My mother never watches movies to understand the essence. She always focuses on the most unimportant parts. That's why it's understandable to me that for her, absolutely all films have a point. A person who doesn't seek the essence doesn't mind not finding it.

"Hey you, come to the window!" the voice from earlier calls out again. At the same time I can hear small pebbles being thrown directly against my window. I get up from the couch and go to check what it is. I don't open the window, but peer through the glass, and look downstairs.

At that moment, a small stone hits the window right in front of my eyes. For that second, I think it is going to hit me, so I open the window angrily, look below, and try to find the culprit.

I see the person responsible. It's the woman in the grey coat. She's dressed in the same coat she wore the previous day, she is smiling, and just as beautiful as I recall. She seems so full of life. She giggles and looks up at me.

"Who are you and what do you want?" I shout.

"Who am I?" she laughs, playfully.

"You have a very loud voice; loud and high-pitched. That's the worst combination. One can hear you even when you are not there," I shout. I expect her to say something, but she just keeps looking at me, and smiles.

"Tell me who you are? What are you looking for under my window?" I shout, straining my voice and getting upset.

"You are very serious, smile a little."

"If you don't tell me who you are and what you want from me, I will close the window and go inside."

"Okay, okay, don't get angry, calm down," she laughs, and it makes me feel self-conscious.

"Do you even know why you're laughing?" I ask, straining hard. I want her to hear me, but I strained so hard I think I might lose my voice.

"I laugh because life is beautiful; and you, why don't you laugh?" she continues in her high-pitched voice. Her voice is impossible to ignore, just like the boring movie I was watching a while ago.

"I don't laugh, because I'm smart enough to know that life can't be beautiful if it isn't easy."

"How sad," she says.

"I'm closing the window. Whoever you are, I'm glad I didn't meet you," I say, trying to close the window.

"Alright," she shouts in that shrill voice, and it seems to me that all the people passing by her stop for a moment.

"Please don't scream at me like that

anymore!" I say.

"I am Leah," she says.

"I am Enzo; and so now what? What do you want from me, Leah?"

"A cigarette; I saw you smoking. I saw you yesterday too."

She says it like I am a small child who did something bad, and who must ask her for forgiveness.

"I saw you yesterday too. It was impossible not to. You walked past me wearing that grey coat, and I still don't understand why you're wearing it. It's hot outside, its summer you know?"

"I know, but I like coats."

"Why?"

"I like it because it's plain. It doesn't reveal anything about my personality or my character, so nobody can make assumptions about me just from looking at me. You know how people are- always judging you from what they see on the outside. I don't want to be judged by superficial things. Almost nobody wants to look deeper than what they see with their eyes. I don't like that, so I like to wear plain things. I hide the core of me, my essence, for those who want to search for it."

I look at her looking at me, not able to

understand what is happening to me. I can't escape the way I'm starting to feel about her. She's absolutely perfect in my eyes. Every one of her dark hairs falls into place, every part of her body seems to move to the rhythm of some beautiful music, and from her gaze it seems a river full of emotion flows. Her energy is so strong and seductive. I look at her impatiently, looking forward to meeting her, and I want to tell her that.

"Leah, there are two things I could not ignore today. The first is the boring film on television and its non-existent point. You are the second thing, the greatest essence, whose core I can see even now, but I fear I will not be able to understand you."

Chapter 2

Leah got under my skin. We meet, and from that day I spend every day with her. She is so deeply ingrained in my consciousness that I don't think I will ever be able to drive her out of my thoughts. I'm fine, and at the same time I'm scared. Everything feels new to me; she takes me to places I didn't even know existed and gives me a completely different view of the world. She complicates my life in one way, yet simply makes me happy in another.

We walk the streets of Pisa; we run; we play; we laugh. We don't touch; we don't kiss; we're not intimate at all, and yet we have something incredibly intimate. We live life. We do everything those people I watched from my window do; those people who I thought were crazy. I don't feel too hot in the sun. I even forget that it's summer. I walk around breathless without realising it. I exist in the moment. I feel like I can change things I don't like, and I find such things beautiful now. Every second I'm happy, every second is different from the previous moment, and for the first time in my life, time passes so fast that I want to pack time into a suitcase to hold it still.

"Are you okay?" Leah asks me.

"I'm fine," I smile with a shy look.

"That is the most important thing, that is what people live for, only for that," she tells me.

The truth is I know absolutely nothing about Leah, except that she is beautiful, young, and irresistibly alive. Time passes too fast and I desperately want to stop it from running away from us. As time ticks, questions form in my mind. I want to know everything about her, yet I feel that I already know everything I need to know.

"How someone makes you feel is the most intimate thing you can know about that person. Everything else is less important," she will say almost every day.

"I agree," I will say, looking at her, "but I am in love with you and I want to know everything about you, even the things that are less important. Is that a sin?" I will mutter when she does not listen to me.

My parents don't know about us, but they can see the changes in me. I think that makes them happy. I'm rarely at home these days. I start to have my own life, and I'm not afraid to live it. At home, my mother regularly gives me little smiles as she sits in the living room or the kitchen, and my father pats me on the shoulder when I go out. I know that means they're happy because they know I'm happy too.

Pisa is still crowded with summer tourists, and the number just keeps growing. I can't believe that Leah and I are pushing through the crowd every day, and I don't even mind it. Leah enjoys it. She's like a feather. She passes through the crowds easily, gently, slipping through. I see the way she moves and I love her even more. I want her. I need her, and it excites me in a strange way.

"Do you want to go to the beach?" she asks me out of the blue. I look at her and feel embarrassed. I can't swim and I don't how to tell her. I act like I'm not interested.

"Where?" I ask. It will be so crowded and surely the water is dirty."

"Anywhere, come let's go to Marina di Pisa. It's so beautiful there," Leah insists.

"I don't know Leah, I don't feel well," I say, although Marina di Pisa is one of the places everyone wants to go to. Who doesn't want to leave the city to go to the beach?

"Come on, why aren't you feeling well? Is there a reason?" she asks, probing.

I have a million reasons why I don't want to go of course, but I don't want to tell her any of them. I'm too shy.

"You know what, you may have your reasons, but you certainly have at least one reason good enough to come with me," she laughs.

I tell myself I have to stop focusing on all the reasons that make me feel scared. Normally when I hesitate to do something, I focus on the reasons why I don't want to do the thing, and those reasons always win. Maybe though, those reasons don't actually win, but I allow them to win.

I smile at Leah and stop arguing. I decide to try something new instead. I decide to go along with her, even though I know that I won't know how to act when we get to the beach, but there is an important reason why I want to go. The reason is that I have never done anything before that was not dictated by my fear. I have always fed my fear, caring for it more than for myself, giving it strength to grow inside me more and more, eventually swallowing me. I decide this time, I will act differently.

Marina di Pisa is only ten kilometres from Pisa. It is a nice small place, with beaches, restaurants, and bars. Tourists love to go there for walks in the harbour. In the summer season the place is full. Everyone goes there to relax and enjoy themselves. Leah gave me instructions on what to bring along, but I felt incredibly nervous.

"Look how wonderful it is, and you didn't want to come! Lucky you have me," Leah says as she laughs, dragging her large, colourful beach bag.

"Where did you get this bag? It's a strange looking bag, and that hat!" I tease her.

"I have a complete set of hats," she says, "didn't you notice?"

"No."

"You see everything, but in fact you don't see anything."

"I only see the surface of things remember.

I'm superficial," I reply, teasing her.

"You're not superficial, you're far from superficial. You're scared of the depth in things, so you float to the surface," she looks at me, and I am speechless. "Here, we can stay here, this is enough space for us, and it's close to the water."

I don't reply. We lie down on my big, green towel. I'm hoping she doesn't bring up going into the water, because it's a conversation I want to avoid.

"Let's go swimming, come on!" she shouts impatiently as she takes off her linen dress, revealing a sexy bathing suit beneath it. The bathing suit barely covers what it needs to.

"Don't you think your swimsuit is too provocative?" I look at her. She is glowing like the sun, ready for play.

"Don't be boring, let's go for a swim!" She runs to the sea like an excited little girl, fearless, not fighting the water but loving it. She folds into the waves naturally, and the sea accepts her as if she were a part of it. It is effortless perfection to watch. She goes in deep, until I can no longer see her.

I try to enjoy the beach and forget about the fact that I don't know how to swim. I stretch out on my green towel and close my eyes. The sun caresses me and I surrender to the warmth. I am sinking into another world. I forget everything. I forget where I am. I feel like a bird in a tropical region. I am colourful and I am painted with the most beautiful, bright shades. It's impossible not to notice me and not to admire me, but I'm different from the other birds. It's a pity, but I don't know how to fly.

I feel droplets of water trickle me in places on my body. I wake up from my wonderful dream, and I see Leah standing beside me, squeezing water from her beautiful, long, dark hair, dripping over me.

"What are you doing?" I ask her.

"Why don't you come in and swim?" she laughs.

"I can't swim," I blurt out.

"There is no such thing," she says.

"There is such a thing. Look, I can't swim."

"I know you can swim, I know. Come on!"

"Leah, stop."

"Come on Enzo, come on."

"Leah, I can't swim, okay. I don't know how to. I don't know how to swim." She looks at me with her blue eyes, as deep as all the seas. She looks at me with a dull stare.

"Why didn't you tell me Enzo? Why hide it

from me?"

"I didn't think it was important."

"It's important. Swimming is important."

"I don't understand you. You're confusing me."

"Swimming is a symbol of fearlessness. Swimming means swimming through problems and through obstacles. It doesn't matter how you swim, but it's important to try. It's important to have a goal and not to give up. It's not about the damn swimming in the sea. It's about swimming through life, through struggle, into truth, into your truth, into what you believe in!"

That's what I love most about Leah. She knows what to say, and she knows how to say what I don't like to hear. She knows how to touch me, and she does it without hurting me.

"I have never even tried," I am embarrassed to say.

"There is no time like the present. Let's try now. I will stand beside you. I promise I will be by your side the whole time, and nothing will happen to you," she extends her hand to me, looking at me with her beautiful eyes, full of sincerity.

We walk to the sea and I put my feet in the water. I can't believe what I'm doing - but I keep going. Leah holds my hand and slowly pulls me forward.

"You won't drown, it's impossible; and do you know why- because, instinctively you'll want to be saved, believe me. You won't let anything bad happen to you," she says.

I listen to her and keep going deeper and deeper. The water hugs me halfway, and I'm afraid, but I don't show it. I keep going in deeper, and I don't turn back. I go forward. Leah is smiling. I focus on her warm face. She gives me strength that I couldn't imagine. The water reaches my neck and Leah starts swimming, still holding onto me with one hand. She does not let me go.

"I will be right here all the time, don't worry, but try to let go Enzo. Try it alone, try. Whatever happens, I'm here. Come on, learn to swim. Learn to depend only on yourself, come on, you can, I know you can."

I can still reach the bottom of the water with my feet. I keep going forward and I know that in a short time, I will not be able to stand. I'm scared, I'm terribly scared, but I try not to think about it. I think of the worst, but then I think of the best. I decide to hope. I close my eyes, and I feel the sun caressing me. I hear Leah's gentle voice.

My feet can't feel the bottom of the water anymore. The water gets too deep to stand, and I let go of Leah's hand. I start moving my arms the way I think I should, and I kick with my legs, trying not to sink. It's hard for me and I swallow some water, my head sinks a little, but I don't give up. I take a breath and move on. I try keeping my head above water in one place, without swimming forward. I kick my feet and somehow I stay on the surface. My arms hurt, my legs hurt even more, but I keep going. I manage to find some balance. I have been alone in the deep sea for a few minutes and I haven't drowned yet. It gives me the strength to move on. I see Leah swimming. She doesn't say anything but I know she's proud of me. I know her silence means she's pleased. I smile. I feel incredible strength and desire. I feel like I'm full of courage. I want to start moving forward, to start swimming, so I kick and use my hands as shovels, scooping and scooping through the water. I breathe. I see the light and I breathe. I inhale oxygen as I scoop water and move. I don't stop. I don't turn back. I focus on my goal. Leah looks at me and waves her hand.

"Congratulations," she shouts. "You learned

to swim!"

I smile, and I'm still doing fine. I keep moving, using my hands as paddles. I keep scooping water like I'm digging a hole in the sea. I'm not fast, but I try. I'm not perfect, but I'm swimming.

Chapter 3

I learned to swim. I can't believe it - I learned to swim! It seems to me that if I continue to listen to Leah, I will learn to fly. It seems that, like a real tropical bird I will be able to spread my wings across the sky, showing off my most beautiful colours. And what is so terrible about flying? The answer is nothing. It would certainly be wonderful to be able to see multiple places from above at the same time, witnessing the beauty that is everywhere. Imagine just waving my wings to rejoice for no particular reason, and to suddenly realise that there is beauty in me too.

I have to admit though, something is bothering

me. I want to ignore it but I can't. It bothers me like a little bug crawling inside my body. It doesn't leave me alone. I can't help myself. I spend more and more time with Leah, and I still know absolutely nothing about her. I can't control myself, and I have so many questions. I am constantly thinking and I have countless dilemmas in my head. I want to know everything about her, but the truth is that I don't know anything about her, not really.

I know I have to talk to her about it. I have to ask her, and she should understand where I'm coming from, if I mean anything to her. My thoughts spin in my head. I don't even know if I mean anything to her. Maybe she just wants us to hang out and spend time together without serious intentions.

No. We are close. I believe in her. I believe in us. I feel like she is mine, even though we just met. I don't know how this is possible, but I know that what is happening is real.

Leah and I walk through the centre of Pisa. We talk about different things and we laugh together. We stop in front of an ice cream shop, and Leah asks me what flavour I like. I tell her I don't care.

"How can you not care about anything in life, not even ice cream?" she says.

"So what, I have no opinions, I don't care."

She goes in and picks ice cream for the two of us, and I wait for her outside. She comes back with ice cream and hands me one, saying, "For you *amarena*, for me *fragola*." She laughs.

"I don't care, Leah," I repeat, taking the ice cream. "The truth is that I'm not familiar with any of the tastes of ice cream, nor do I know which taste I would prefer." I pause as we walk. "Leah, I want to talk about something," I say, licking the ice cream and walking.

"Don't you like your ice cream?"

She looks at me with a question mark on her face.

"No, it's wonderful. I like it very much. It's not that," I smile. "In fact, I don't really care about the ice cream because I'm not interested in ice cream. I want to talk about something else. I want to talk about us, about you," I say. "Leah, I know nothing about you, absolutely nothing. All I know is that your name is Leah, and that's not enough for me anymore. I want to know you, do you understand me? I need information. I want to know details about you. I want to know small things, specifics. I have a lot of questions in my head that I want answered."

"Yes, that's your biggest problem," she says nonchalantly, more focused on her ice cream than on our conversation.

"Why do you think that is my biggest problem, I don't understand," I ask her, confused.

"Because you want to spend your time like that, and I know that it torments you constantly. Your life is taken up with asking a million questions, and not getting answers to them. All this ultimately results in is your own disappointment, which prevents you from living life. It takes away the pleasure of enjoying moments, and makes you forget how happy you actually are, and then you miss out on everything. You miss out on everything that happens to you because you're only thinking about what you don't have, and what didn't happen. You miss out on being happy in the moment. That is the greatest proof that nothing is yours to enjoy, and the answers to all the questions that you so desperately need, are only an illusion and a trap, and you don't need them at all."

I shut my mouth because I know she's right. The problem is I also know that it's not enough for her to be right. I know that even now, even if I agree with her and promise her that I will never raise this topic, this conversation again - I will suffer because of it.

"Okay Leah, you're right, but I still want to know everything. You just can't change my mind like that."

"And you are right Enzo, only you can change it," she smiles at me. "The more you know things, the more you don't know them at all. Do you understand? There is only this moment and all you can do is exist in it."

In an unexpected flash, a huge crowd of people swarm onto the walkway. Leah grabs me by the arm and leads me through it. She is magical. I don't know how she does this. We avoid the frenzy of the crowd and keep walking. We talk about other things. The weather is always too hot in summer, but the sun is now slowly setting. We reach the Piazza Martiri della Liberta and sit down on one of the marble benches. We never run out of things to say and the conversation is beautiful.

Leah asks me if I know this place very well, and I tell her that it is actually one of my favourite places in Pisa. We chat some more and she touches my hand, squeezes it affectionately, and looks at me.

"I want to tell you something about myself," she says.

"No, you don't have to, really," I say, assuming now that she feels pressured.

"No," she looks at me with her beautiful blue eyes, and I see a million tears gathered up in them. I have never seen Leah like this before. I don't understand it.

"Enzo, I know you've wanted to know more about me for some time now. I still think you already know a lot more than I can tell you. But I'm ready to talk about myself a little," she pauses then continues, "Enzo, before I met you, I was a very free woman," she says, looking at me.

"Free? What do you mean? I don't understand," I say.

"Free. I have always been like that. I'm still like that. I want to live life. I'm the kind of person who does what makes her happy in the moment. I want new experiences and I want to make mistakes too, because I want to learn from my own mistakes."

"I still don't understand you."

"I don't even know why I'm telling you this, but I feel I need to share some things with you. I think you can learn something new from it too. I think you are filled with prejudice and anger, and I think it can destroy you."

"Leah, will you tell me what you are talking about?"

"Enzo, when you first saw me from your terrace in my grey coat, where do you think I came from?"

"I don't know. How would I know?"

"Enzo, I was on my way back from someone's place, a man's home. I slept there. That's why I wore the coat, because of the clothes I had on underneath it."

I have no answer to this so I stay silent.

"This is something personal I'm telling you, but I want you to know," she says.

"So you sleep with men?" I ask her.

"Yes, I sleep with men if I want to sleep with them. I am the kind of person who does what she wants. I make mistakes, I often make mistakes, but I don't regret anything. The person I am today was created through all the things that happened to me," she says, and I continue to be silent. "Why are you looking at me like that?" she says in a defensive tone. "Don't you believe me? Does what I told you make me a bad person?"

"That makes you a prostitute, Leah," I shout at her, struggling to find my objectivity. The words simply spew out of me.

"A prostitute?" she shouts. "Call the newspapers then! I don't think I can be labelled a prostitute; and even if I am one, I am not just that, I am many other things, do you understand me? Who gives you the right to judge anyone? It is complex. A person is never just one thing. People go through different phases in life, people change. There are wonderful people who don't have spotless pasts, and there are many bad people with a flawless history. Those things are unrelated. What matters is how someone makes you feel, and everything else is irrelevant. We should forget about all the labels, all the name-calling, and the stereotypes. Labels are problems we create for ourselves, and it prevents us from truly understanding the purpose of our existence," she said. She pauses and looks at me. "Are you disappointed?" she asks.

"So when I first saw you in the grey coat, were you coming back from someone's house?"

"Yes."

"You were wearing provocative clothes under your coat, clothes you had to hide?"

"I told you that's why I love plain coats

because it doesn't give away any clues. It could mean anything or nothing because it leaves no impressions. The coat is not important, and the clothes under the coat are even less important. Neither one of it is me. The essence of who I am is completely different. The essence of me is for those who can really see me.

"You are ashamed of yourself, is that why you hide behind a coat?"

"No. Why do you think I'm hiding?"

"So why do you pretend to be something else then? Why didn't you confess who you are immediately? Why do you want someone to love you without knowing you?" I can't hold myself back from attacking her, even though I don't want to hurt her.

"I told you because I'm not just one thing. I'm Leah - this or that does not define who I am, it has nothing to do with my heart and my soul," she says with tears beginning to fall, and lowering her head.

I knew I was going to hurt her, even though I didn't want to hurt her. I go quiet for a while. I sit there speechless. I just don't know what to say.

"All right, Enzo, that's how you choose to look at the world, and I don't want to take your perspective away from you. I just want to tell you something. If your theory is correct, if people are exactly what they did and what happened to them, and if people's deeds are the core of who they are; if words are just a desperate way to escape out of that core- then who are you?"

She gets up and begins to walk away. I sit on the marble bench in Piazza Martiri della Liberta, alone, without her, watching her get lost in the distance. I begin to feel her absence strongly. The beautiful Leah is gone. I lose the only light I have to brighten the darkness, the doubt, and all the cruelty of this world.

Chapter 4

"Doctor, we have seen some unexpected signs of improvement. The change is almost unbelievable."

"Yes, it's definitely unexpected. He's strong, but he's been locked up for a long time and has his guard up."

"What now? How do we deal with him?"

"Be the same as you were before, Nurse. Observe, analyse, help, and pay attention. If his condition worsens, you know what to give him."

"Yes."

"Remember, this is not our fight. It's his."

"We are afraid for him at times. When he is

aware of himself, it's like something hurts him, and we don't know how to help."

"Don't be afraid, it's good. The pain is good. Something is happening, something is changing for him."

"Is he changing?"

"The world in which he lives must change, and once it changes it will fall apart. Only his decaying world can give him a whole new world. Only his decaying world can give him a better world."

.   .   .

Time passes. I get a little stronger and come home again. I'm doing the same things I did before I met Leah. I haven't seen her for several days. She didn't ask about me, but I stand at my window searching. I don't see her. Maybe life took her somewhere else. Maybe now she is with a man who lives on the other side of town. I can't believe I'm thinking about it again and discussing it with myself.

Leah will never forgive me for thinking of her that way. I want to understand what she meant when she said she doesn't feel like a prostitute. How can she not feel like one when she does those things? Maybe I should have asked her more questions, tried to understand her, and been curious. Maybe I should have asked her why she was doing it, and maybe she would have given me some big reason to justify her decision in my eyes. Maybe she would tell me that she had a difficult childhood, that her father left her when she was little, and that her mother died of grief a year later. Maybe she would have told me something so sad that I would have felt sorry for her and understood her. I don't want to judge her, but she must give me a good reason. She didn't even try to explain it to me. She didn't even try to convince me. She should have been a little more interested in getting me to look at the situation fairly. She should have fought for my understanding.

It's Monday now, and it's another boring day. I open my eyes, and I don't even know why I get up. Every new day I lie to myself that the next day something will happen that will make me feel better, but it doesn't happen. I'm not that strong, that much is obvious. I even think I'm weaker than I was before I met her. She gave me some strength, and then seemed to take away all the strength I ever had in myself.

"What should I do with myself today?" I murmur this as I smoke a cigarette at my window. I am stuck in a void, and I can't focus on anything. The feeling is awful. I can't find anything that will interest me, no matter how much I wish I could. I feel like I don't exist.

"Enzo, you haven't been looking for me all week!" Leah's voice echoes from somewhere. I try to find her, I look for her, but I can't see her.

"Where are you?" I shout and panic, feeling that I'm losing her all over again.

"Look under the window, right under the window!" she laughs. "You never seem to learn that the things we look for are often right in front of our noses!"

She laughs with her high-pitched voice that I miss so much. I look for her somewhere far away. My gaze wanders between all the people, not realising that the voice is coming from close by; not realising that what I'm looking for is right in front of me. I see her. I really see her. She is standing under my window. I feel different the moment she appears. I start breathing when I look into Leah's eyes, and laugh along with her.

"I was looking for you in my own way. Why didn't you ask for me?" I shout.

"I didn't know if you wanted to be asked about by someone like me," she screams out loud, not caring who hears her.

I want to scold her for screaming, but the moment I open my mouth to rebuke her, I realise that I'm the one who deserves rebuking, and I feel ashamed of myself.

"You are Leah!" I shout aloud.

She looks at me in surprise, as if she thinks I don't trust her. Her eyes though– the whole world for me exists in her eyes.

"Am I Leah?" she says, trying to dig into me somewhat. She is modest but at the same time completely confident, dignified, and incredibly real.

"You are Leah!" I yell at her as hard as I can. I close the window, run to the front door, and out of the building. I pull her into my arms and hold her there. I hold her like a man holds a woman, and she looks at me with those beautiful eyes. I kiss her all over her beautiful face, on her soft mouth, and on her long neck. I hold her and don't let her go.

"Do you like my scent? I have a new perfume," she says with a laugh. "I really like it on me. I always want to smell like this. I want you to smell like this. I want our world to smell like this; always."

I remove her soft hair from her delicate face. I

wrap my arms around her waist and bring her closer to me.

"I don't know about the scent," I say, "but you will always smell like home to me."

Chapter 5

Leah and I spend a lot of time together and I already feel like I know everything about her. We build our world. She wanted that world to smell like perfume, so we stopped smoking cigarettes, and we don't miss it at all. The scent of Leah completely fills every gap in my life.

We overcome any difficulties together. We meet each other with grace, without expectations or prejudices. We begin to feel, and I begin to believe less and less in my own annoying questions and constant doubts. We talk about life openly, even though talking is something I never practiced, but avoided. I didn't think talking could lead to any solutions, and it's hard for me to change that part of myself, but I try. I love our incredibly real and productive conversations and become increasingly aware that people lack just that - communication.

Leah is my motivation to change and become a better person. She possesses a strange power to encourage me to do the right thing, without forcing me. I remember my mother's words. She always says she is not a wise woman because all her life she pointed out my father's mistakes to him and made him listen to her. She says this is why he never obeyed her. I agree with her. People shouldn't be like that. The essence of pointing things out is directly related to the fear of those to whom we point it out to.

Everything is in my hands but pointing out what I do wrong is a way of scaring me into obeying you, and therefore a way of tying my hands. I will never listen to you and give you results, even if I want to- I will not be able to, because my hands are tied. So untie my hands and let me move them freely as I wish. Let me make mistakes, let me fall, let me grow. You just need to be here and believe in me. Life will create situations for which I am ready, and I will be able to realise when I was wrong, but don't force me there. Wait for me, and we will arrive soon.

It's my birthday in less than a week, and I'm turning thirty years old. All the people I know in Pisa assess life by using before and after thirty years old as a benchmark. It's difficult to stay immune to stereotypes. You try to avoid them but you are already part of them. People talk a lot and people ask a lot of questions. I usually have nothing to say to them. At times I wish I were part of the crowd. At times I think everything would be a lot easier that way, but since I met Leah I try not to think about it too much, and then it gets easier. My life is divided into many parts, and many times I thought my end had come, but from the moment Leah came into my life I count only the days I feel alive.

"Enzo, what do you want for your birthday?" she asks me with a laugh as we walk, even though I told her several times that I don't want a present.

"I told you, I don't want anything, really."

"I'm serious. Imagine I have all the money in the world and can buy you literally anything. What would you like for your birthday then?" she says, playing with her long hair, and looking down at her shoes.

"I would like to buy you a pair of new shoes, and for you to give your old shoes to me as a birthday present," I say, pointing at them.

"You mean my shoes are old? I have other shoes, of course I do, but you know how it is. When you get used to a pair of shoes, you wear it until it's worn out", she laughs. When she smiles at me like that, it makes me feel that there is nothing terrible in this world and that everything can be overcome. Feeling light, I begin to believe that we may have been given this life to enjoy it after all, and not to suffer.

"That is not my point. I didn't want to offend you," I look at her anxiously, fearing that she misunderstood me. "I just want to buy you the most beautiful shoes in the world, and you can give me yours for your birthday, can I?"

"But I really don't understand you. What will you do with an old pair of woman's shoes?" she looks at me confused.

" Your shoes are only worn, not old. They are not only women's shoes either, but yours. I want to know what it's like to be in your shoes, I want to feel it. You know, when I first saw you, I thought you could barely walk in those shoes, but I was wrong, because a minute later I saw you running in them. I need your shoes, to put them in my room and to look at them every time I think I have the right to underestimate you."

"To underestimate me?" she asks.

"Yes. I will surely underestimate you some day, and when that happens, I want to have your shoes in front of my eyes, so that I can help myself to believe in you again, and not allow myself to go back to the way I was, that dark, hopeless alley where I was desperately unhappy."

She looks at me and laughs, and I know we understand each other.

"All right Enzo, on your birthday you will get my shoes."

"I can't wait."

"I know what I can't wait for," she says, coming close to my face, looking me straight in the eyes with a childish smile.

"What?"

I kiss her. It is as lovely as the taste of freshly baked cake.

"I can't wait to have new shoes!" she laughs out loud. "Come on, let's go, we don't have much time, we have to choose new shoes! Get up!"

She pulls me by the arm and we start running. I don't know where we're headed. All I know is that we need to find a new pair of shoes. I don't know how long it will take to find a pair either. Maybe Leah is infinitely indecisive when it comes to choosing shoes. Maybe I will get tired and disappoint her by telling her I no longer have the strength to look for the perfect pair of shoes. Maybe all the tourists in Pisa have already bought the most beautiful shoes, and only the ugly ones are left. Maybe there are no shoes that are worthy of a woman like Leah, other than the ones she already wore on her feet for a while, turning them into real ones.

.

Chapter 6

It's my birthday and I am thirty years old. I don't feel that age, I just feel happy. Leah and I will go to the beach today, to the same place where I learned to swim, and then we will sit in a restaurant and have dinner. We agreed to have a day full of activities and to enjoy the time we spend together. I am in an exceptionally good mood, and I am very happy. I have never been so happy on my birthday before. When I was little, I celebrated my birthday because my parents wanted me to, and when I was old enough to celebrate it alone, I had no desire to. My mother always buys me a birthday cake, and my father wishes the same wishes for me every year.

Over time, his voice begins to feel more impatient with me, but this year everything is different. It's always hot outside for my birthday, and I can't change that because I was born in August. Today I don't mind at all.

Leah was born in February, and I asked her several times what it feels like to be born in winter. She tells me that it's exactly the same as when I was born, and that what matters is that you came into this world, that you were born at all. I agree with her. I don't want to get into an argument or discussion about it, but I try to learn something new every day. I realise how powerful that is. The process of resisting and rejecting the unknown is tedious and exhausting, but the process of informing and encouraging one's own learning is incredibly useful.

We head to Marina di Pisa. Leah is carrying a large, straw picnic basket with a few things packed in it. I immediately think she is hiding the shoes she promised to give me in her picnic basket. At the same time, I think of the new shoes that I promised to give her. I'm disappointed because after a few hours of searching for the perfect shoes, we give up. Leah told me that some things should not be forced.

"In life, things happen when the time is right, Enzo. You must not lose hope, but you should not expect everything to happen when you want it to," she says after we decide to abandon the search for her new pair of shoes, leaving it for another time.

I hear her, but I can't stop thinking that Leah is probably disappointed in me for not getting the shoes on the same day. I am overwhelmed by the thought that she may believe that I never really wanted to get her those shoes, but that I just agreed and secretly hoped we would not find them, so I wouldn't need to buy them after all. I don't want her to think that I'm frivolous.

Life is strange. When I have the most serious intention, I act as if I don't know what I'm doing. Still, I hope she's right, maybe things really do happen when the time is right. Maybe one day, when we forget about the shoes, we will find them, as Leah said.

We arrive in Marina di Pisa.

"Enzo, look how many people there are here. Enzo!" She is excited seeing the huge crowd on the beach. "Imagine, all these people coming to this beach to celebrate your birthday with us!"

"But I know they didn't come because of that," I look at her confused.

"But just imagine they did. It doesn't matter why they came, imagine that they came because of you and let it be!" she giggles, falling onto the sand.

"Shall we sit here?" I ask her, looking at a clean spot on the sand.

"Yes; here, there, anywhere- it's beautiful everywhere!" she continues to giggle and unpacks her picnic basket.

Although it's not so funny to me, I accept being a part of her game and throw the towel down on the sand. I lie on it and look up at the sky. I take a deep breath, and the sun caresses my body. For a moment, I stop thinking so much. I take in how beautiful Leah is, and how her energy calms me. I love her spontaneity and her nonchalance, although it is very difficult for me to understand all the time. I turn and look at her. She strokes her hair and sprays suntan lotion over her skin. She is so sweet, so beautiful, and so real.

"Leah, be spontaneous, grab life!" I giggle to her.

"You?!" she looks at me. "Are you telling me that?!"

"Do you see how things can change when you have the right person by your side, and how you can see things that you never thought you would be able to see?" I keep giggling.

"Enzo, my dear Enzo, all the beautiful things that happen to you, happen to you thanks to yourself. Please do not forget that," she looks at me and kisses me gently.

As she touches me, I feel an electric energy trickling through me. It is a feeling I haven't felt with another woman. What is she doing to me? I don't understand what's happening to me. She and I have always kept some boundaries, some barriers, and I feel comfortable that way. I like it when there are restrictions, but if you must be spontaneous and grab life to enjoy it, then why not me too? I want to get out of the old habits holding me back. I want to do things I have been afraid to do, to become someone I have never been before, but could be.

Leah moves closer to me, caresses me all over my body, kisses me, and whispers to me.

"It's a shame there are people here, really, but tonight we will find a place where we can be alone, just you and I."

I'm still struggling. I have to face the truth. The truth is I want her, but I'm not sure I am comfortable enough to show it. I don't know how to show it. I have no experience with such things. I have no experience at all.

"Leah, I ...," I murmur shyly.

"I know, everything is clear to me," she says. She sounds so confident.

"Do you understand what I'm afraid of?" I ask in disbelief.

"Yes, and we will get past that. We will do it together."

I'm silent. I see her. I want her. I love her. I love her with all of my small, wounded, and inexperienced heart.

. . .

"What's the matter with him doctor, what happened? Explain it to us. Please explain it to us, nothing makes sense."

"The situation has deteriorated, Mr. and Mrs. Moretti. We don't know why exactly, but his condition has changed. Unfortunately in such situations, anything can happen."

"Yes, but we don't understand. We do not understand what is happening!"

"Look, we are doing our best, and it really looked like he was getting better, I was sure we were on the right track, but you must understand, we are only doctors. In the end, this is his battle to win. He has to fight. I felt something with him earlier... I felt a change in him..."

"What do you mean a change? Tell us, what change doctor?"

"Only he knows that for sure, but I'm sure of one thing– he's fighting. He's fighting with his greatest enemy –and that is himself. Each time he is hurt, he withdraws, but trust me, he will come back to finish this fight. He is alive, and for the first time after a long time I can see it in his eyes, he wants to live."

Chapter 7

I open my eyes and immediately think of Leah and how good my birthday was. It makes me smile and think I will never forget that day. She made me feel so happy. We talked about everything, and she understood me. Leah is the kind of person who never makes me uncomfortable, and if she accidentally does something I don't like, she knows when to stop. We watched the sunset, we enjoyed being together, we ate, we bathed, we kissed, and I swam. I swam as far as I could, and she did not force me to go any further.

"There is a right time for everything," she

said.

Today is an especially important day for me because Leah and I are going to Migliarino, San Rossore, Massaciuccoli National Park. The Park is part of the province of Pisa, and according to everyone who visits it, it is a real experience. It is rich in beautiful flora and fauna. You can go for a walk, a picnic, ride a bike, ride a horse, ride a boat on the ponds, taste wonderful food and wine, play sport, or enjoy the beaches.

The Park is popular with tourists, and many of them spend all day there. Although I'm from Pisa, I've never been, and Leah has been many times. She told me that the Park is one of her favourite places and she really wants us to go there together. After a while I give in and agree to visit it.

I really don't want to disappoint Leah. I want to have a good time; to have fun and relax. I want us to enjoy each other's company and I want to make her happy. I've never wanted to be a source of negativity to anyone; I hate it when I'm ruining someone's day, and I've often done it unintentionally. That makes this day very important to me. I'm going to a new place and I'm going to experience new things. I want everything to be more than fine. I want it to be wonderful.

"I'm very excited Enzo; very!" Leah says on the way to the Park.

"Me too," I smile.

"You'll see how beautiful this Park is Enzo; how calming it is. It's magical! You'll feel wonderful - nature heals you, nature helps you and saves you," she says.

The truth is I'm afraid. I'm sure the Park is beautiful, but it's probably crowded. There must be countless numbers of tourists, and noise everywhere. The Park has limited space with limited room for movement, and limited activities. In the Park all people are cheerful, smiling, and full of life. It scares me. It really scares me that I might disappoint Leah.

"Here we are, here we are!" she screams with joy.

She is so excited about this day. I know that she understands me, but what if the day comes when she doesn't understand me anymore and thinks it is time for her to give up on me? What if I don't fit into this new place the way she wants me to? What if I don't fit into her idea of how she wants me to be? I don't want to disappoint her. I don't want to hurt her. I couldn't stand it, but yet I keep pushing myself down into this hole.

I'm only afraid of myself, no one else. I don't want to face this situation. I don't want to look at myself too closely. I don't want to put myself in a scenario where things are expected of me. I'm damn scared I won't meet those expectations. Fear seizes me and doesn't let me go. I feel like I don't belong here, like I don't belong in the regular world, with people who do regular things and function normally.

I feel lost when I can't give people the reaction they want from me, and that frustrates me even more. I feel the world's eyes looking at me strangely. It crawls like ants and tickles me. It is impossible to ignore. It is impossible not to notice. I'm convinced that we are not all the same, and that we aren't all supposed to live the same life. This is why I don't want to go to places where I might not fit in. I don't want to lie to people. I don't want anyone to suffer because of me; that was never my intention.

I can't bear to see disappointment in Leah's beautiful eyes; my guide; my only light; my serenity and perfect silence. I can't bear to disappoint her. I won't forgive myself for that. I'm not good enough. I'm not strong enough. I'm not big enough. I'm very small, and I only do small things, make small changes, and do small deeds. I can only do that much.

I want to smile too, but it's hard for me.

"Come on, come on, let's go in," she says.

I break into a cold sweat and I think I will die. No. I know I will not die, I will just suffer, and that is scarier.

We enter. The Park is incredibly beautiful.

"Look how wonderful it is, look! Do you feel that? The whole world is ours. Do you feel that we're free, and that we can do whatever we want?" she says and turns in a circle as if there is no one around us.

There are a lot of people but everyone is busy with their own affairs. Some are taking pictures, some are having a picnic on the grass, and others are pushing babies in a stroller. We are standing still while Leah looks around. I'm waiting for her to decide what to do and where to go.

"I think we should rent bicycles," Leah says.

I look at her and say nothing. I haven't been on a bicycle in a long time, although when I was a little boy I loved to ride my four-wheel bike.

"I haven't been on a bike in a long time. Do you think it's a good idea?" I look at her shyly.

"I think it's a great idea! The Park is big and we want to see it all! We won't be able to walk around this entire place, and the boat limits the places we can get to as well. Let's get bikes! It will be fun Enzo, and if we get tired, we can always stop, right? It's up to us. We'll do as we want! Come on Enzo, come on!"

She pulls me to the bicycle rental place and convinces me. I surrender.

"All right, all right, we'll ride bikes."

The temperatures are high but the Park is not really hot. It's a pleasant day, and a gentle breeze blows the greenery around us, killing the heat. We get on our bikes and I notice the dust on the seats. I want to comment about it, but I know if I do it will ruin the moment, so I keep quiet. I get on the bike and we ride off. I thought I would have difficulty riding again, because I haven't been on a bike for a long time. To my surprise, I do great, almost like I never even stopped.

"Leah, look how well I'm riding, and I haven't been on a bike in so long!

Unbelievable!"

"Enzo, that's not amazing at all!" she screams from her bicycle. "You know, we can get back to our happiness very easily if we wish. What prevents us from doing it is the fear that it won't be easy. That's all. See, you once rode a bike and it made you happy. That's why it's easy for you to get back to where you ended off, no matter how much time has passed, because cycling made you happy. Your mind remembers your happiness, your body too."

I keep riding my bike and thinking about what Leah told me.

"What about the sadness?" I ask her.

"What sadness?" she looks at me confused.

"Yes. Does my mind and body remember grief?"

She stops riding and stands her bike in front of me, blocking my path. I almost fall, but I manage to stop too. She parks her bike and walks over to me, looks at me, but says nothing. I feel her breathing anxiously and I think I may have asked a question I shouldn't have asked.

"No, Enzo. Only you remember the sadness," she touches my chest with her hand. It's only you that remembers, and no one else. Do you know why? It's because your mind and your body aren't so naïve as to remember bad things and return to it. Your mind wants to fly, your body wants to dance, and only you want to talk about grief. Only you, without asking, bring sorrow to them, accumulate it in your mind and give it to your body. Only you take the sadness back and only you open the door for it every time it knocks."

I bow my head and don't know what to say. I take her hand and place it on the left side of my chest.

"And this?" I ask, looking her in her eyes.

She looks at me too, but her beautiful face doesn't laugh.

"This Enzo ...," she leans her head onto my shoulders and sighs, "unfortunately, this here will be sad, as long as you are sad. Even if I were here in place of this - here, you would be angry."

She kisses me on the cheek and gets on her bike. She looks at me and smiles bravely, as if everything will be fine. I smile too, as if I think everything will be fine. After all, I trust her.

"Are you ready for this adventure?! Shall we go? I'm ready," she laughs, and we ride our bikes again.

While riding, I think about how easy it is to have a tough conversation with her, and then just keep riding a bike like it wasn't tough at all.

Everything I see is beautiful. Nature is beautiful. The Park is beautiful. I breathe very easily and I find some peace. Birds fly around us, and I see unique plants. I see a wild boar. The Park is home to deer and other animals too. We ride along the path through the forest, and beside us there is a peaceful lake with sailboats. They sell drinks, food, balloons, and all sorts of other things, almost every step of the way. I see small restaurants, people enjoying delicious food, and a glass of wine.

"They have a wonderful local wine here, Enzo. The food is so good too. We'll try it later," Leah yells at me.

We continue riding, and for a moment my eyes fall on a small child playing with a ball. I look at him. He is carefree; laughing, and playing, acting as if he doesn't think of anything else at all. He is fully present in the moment, and completely focused on what is happening to him. I think about that and I don't know how I feel. I don't know what it feels like to be present, and I can't remember the last time I was so engaged in the moment. I am usually present only briefly, before I get lost again. Leah is my anchor; she definitely knows how to station me in one place, at one point.

She teaches me to experience what is happening to me. Surely it would be wonderful to be like that all the time; to exist without any complications, to exist simply, with all your moments experienced fully.

"Enzo, let's take a break. Do you want to?"

Leah asks me.

She can barely breathe and is clearly tired.

"Here, here, on this bench. Let's sit down for a while, look at the sky, and get our strength back."

We stop our bikes and sit on the bench. There is beautiful greenery and birds are singing around us. It is peaceful and perfect. I look at Leah as she ties her sneakers. I look around and I think about everything. This is everything a person needs to be happy. People live for moments like these. I want to live this moment fully, to feel it with every part of my body. I want to be grateful. I want to be aware of what is happening around me. I close my eyes and free myself completely.

"Enzo, look, they are kayaking! Do you know how to kayak?" she asks me.

I don't want to answer her because I feel completely at peace, and I don't want to spoil the moment.

"Enzo, are you sleeping?" she asks, touching my shoulder anxiously.

I open my eyes and look at her.

"Of course not Leah, I'm just relaxing," I say, and she laughs.

"Enzo, I want to talk about something."

"Yes; what about?" I ask anxiously.

"Not now, not here. Later, at lunch, when we sit down; agreed?"

"Yes, yes," I answer feeling confused, not knowing what else to say.

"Come on, we'll ride a little further and then sit down in one of the restaurants. I told you, food and wine are a real experience here. You will fall in love!" she says, pulling me by the arm.

We get up from the bench and get back on our bikes. I still can't believe how easily I fell back into riding bike. Leah is right, happiness is not forgotten. I pedal. I go left. I go right. I have amazing balance, like a real professional. I'm glad there's something I haven't forgotten to do, and that I'm still doing it well. It's not a feeling I feel every day.

At the same time, I can't stop thinking about what Leah said, and suddenly, I'm worried. I can't even imagine what she wants to talk about or what she wants to tell me. Maybe she's bored; maybe she wants to leave me; maybe she's angry at me. I think of the worst. I don't know, but whatever she tells me, I know I will have to understand it. I love her. I love her too much, and I feel it so strongly right now. There are so many beautiful things Leah brought me, so many new horizons I saw, thanks to her. I feel wonderful because of her; because of how beautiful she is, how good she is, how special she is! I watch her ride her bike, with her dark brown hair fluttering carefree. She smiles, enjoying every moment with incredible elegance and lightness. I feel happy looking at her. It makes me feel that I can understand life.

"Enzo, I'm hungry, I can't anymore. Are you hungry?" she interrupts me as I dream.

"Yes, yes," I smile.

"Well, there is a restaurant over there at the end, it must be good. I haven't been to this one,, but everything here is good. Are we going?"

I agree and laugh, racing ahead with my bike. She pedals faster, but she can't catch up. I'm sure she thinks I'm showing off. In fact, I'm just starting to run away, hoping that by riding fast, I can avoid the conversation that follows. I want to escape from something that hasn't happened yet. That's my biggest problem. I hurt because of the past. I live for the future and run away from the present. I run away from the things that haven't happened. I think about moments I haven't experienced yet, I am afraid of my own fears, and I miss everything else. Fearing that something else might happen to me, I miss everything that happens in the meantime.

I can't judge if what is happening to me is good or bad. I can't recount moments, due to my constant absence. I live taking care of someone else's life, and miss this life, not knowing what to do. All I want is to be like the child I just saw. I want to be alive in every moment, and I don't want the fact that I think my world is falling apart, to take the moment away from me. I want to be aware that the world will fall apart without worrying about it, and knowing that even if it does, I can always build a new world; a better and more colourful one.

We leave our bikes outside and go into the restaurant. At the entrance, a gentlemanly waiter greets us and asks if we want to eat or if we just want to have a drink. He seats us at a beautiful table, with a magical view of the lake and the forest. The atmosphere in the restaurant is pleasant, and the sun is shyly starting to recede. Leah's face looks perfect. I see her more clearly than ever, and the gentle breeze seems to pamper her beauty even more. I adore her. The waiter comes to our table and addresses us politely.

"Welcome to our restaurant. What would you like to start with? Can I recommend a good homemade wine?"

"Yes please," Leah says. "We know the wines here are wonderful and you have a really big variety."

"Would you like white, red, or perhaps rose?"

"White please, it's perfect for this time of day, isn't it?" Leah says. I just smile. I really don't know much about the subject and I don't want to say something that will embarrass Leah.

Leah looks at me with a certain look, and for a moment I'm sure I did something wrong.

"Are you okay?" she asks me.

"Yes," I answer.

"No, really, are you okay?"

"Yes."

"Please remember this moment. Please look around and remember this day, this place, the feelings you feel right now, the energy, this wonderful restaurant, the wonderful wine, and the delicious food you will try, please remember everything. Will you try?" she tells me.

"I will try," I tell her.

The waiter brings the wine and Leah immediately orders a selection of cheese and bread. It looks incredibly good.

"Wine and cheese, there's no better combination, right?" she says.

"I wouldn't know," I say.

"Haven't you tried wine and cheese?" She looks at me in astonishment.

"No," I say, feeling embarrassed.

"I can't believe it!" she smiles in astonishment. "All right then, today you will officially lose your innocence. Come on, hello!"

She raises her glass.

. . .

"Enzo! Enzo! Do you hear me? Enzo, are you listening to me? He's not listening to me, sisters, bring something to calm him down, bring something!

"What happened to him, Doctor? Did we lose him again?"

"It's like he is walking on a perfectly flat road, and suddenly someone throws a stone at him, and he stumbles. Enzo, dear child, you must learn to walk on stones. What are you afraid of, Enzo?"

Chapter 8

I wake up feeling incredibly happy because my thoughts are still in the beautiful Park. In front of my eyes I see Leah's long hair. She looks at me with her penetrating eyes, laughing at me so sincerely and clearly.

The walk in the Park was a wonderful experience. We enjoyed every second, and despite all my fears, I somehow managed to indulge in the beauty of nature and the positive energy that Leah always gives me. Cycling tired us out so much, at one point we decided it was time to leave.

Although Leah wanted to talk about

something, she said we would talk about it another time. I still don't know what she wants to talk about, and I'm still a little scared about it, but I try not to think about it.

I focus on positivity. I secretly hope that the conversation will not even happen.

I can't wait to see Leah today. I think of how happy I am to wake up with such joy, with such excitement. I feel that everything around me has a point and has meaning. I feel that my existence is good. This is different from how I usually feel. It is a wonderful feeling. It makes you feel alive.

To live without such a feeling, you die while you are alive. Time passes so slowly when you feel like that, and you see the world with empty eyes. In my world all clocks stopped. They didn't move. I didn't know if I could fix them. I didn't even try. I was used to the silence. Then Leah appeared.

I warned her to be careful, because silence is contagious, and she boldly replied, "Smiling is contagious too."

Leah told me she wants us to go dancing today. We'll go somewhere where there's loud music and lots of people. I'm embarrassed when she suggests things to me because I haven't done most things. I feel stupid because I haven't been anywhere. I hadn't danced, I didn't know how to swim. I'm really ashamed of that.

Leah encourages me and wants to take me to all those places to teach me new things. She has patience with me and I appreciate that the most. I realised that in life people like Leah are really rare. Everyone wants to dance with you, but no one wants to teach you. Everyone wants to swim with you, but no one has the patience to show you how. Everyone wants to go to places with you, but only if you are fun enough and don't spoil the atmosphere. Nobody loves you if you don't fit in with what's popular. People put you in a certain category with incredible ease.

They put you in an old, dusty box, as if you are an object that has broken down - as if you are an object that no longer does its job and is not needed by anyone anymore. It's all sad. The saddest thing is that I wanted to believe, every day I wanted to believe - until I got to the point where I wanted to believe, but I just couldn't.

My parents are at home today, hanging around me. It seems they had no urgent work responsibilities, so they decided to stay home. I look at them and think - my parents are good, they are really good. I know they want the best for me, but I'm sorry they don't know what's best for me. I don't blame them. I've always been quiet, not much of a talker. It may be my fault.

It's not their responsibility to understand what I don't tell them. It really isn't. I want to overcome my pain, and when I get past it, maybe I'll talk about it then. I need time. I don't even know why I'm thinking about all of this now, but as I watch my parents hover around me, I am assaulted by other thoughts.

Other thoughts drag me into another world; a world in which I'm not sure I want to be right now. My world is made up of Leah these days, and it's the only world that exists for me. There may be a million other worlds, there may be better worlds, but what matters is the world I want to be in. My favourite world is called Leah, and that is my biggest truth.

My parents finally go out to buy something. I go to my room to get ready. I'm nervous. Leah told me to get a little dressed up, and I really don't know what to wear. I haven't dressed for a long time, and that's not good. Leah knows that about me, but I still feel some discomfort. I look in the mirror and try to find something that will suit me. I am wearing an old white shirt that I love very much, but I haven't worn it more than twice. It doesn't suit me like it did before. I've changed. I don't know what to do. I don't know how I will go out like this. I wear jeans, which I also like very much, but they don't look the same on me as they looked on me before.

"I can't believe it," I say to myself. "How long since I looked in the mirror? How long since I've taken care of my appearance?!"

I should be embarrassed. I should really be ashamed. I don't know how I can go on like this. The jeans feel as if it were not mine, all the clothes feel as if it were not mine, as if it were borrowed by me, from another person - by another Enzo, who I no longer am. That hurts me.

"What should I do now?!" I mutter and tremble.

I kneel in front of the mirror.

"I will embarrass her if I appear like this. I can't appear like this. My place is not there, that's obvious. My place is not at a party, between happy people, between smiling faces. I will never fit in. I will always stand out. The most ordinary things look strange on me. I don't know how to do anything right. I'm just not normal!" I cry.

The building's doorbell rings. It must be Leah. I am in tears, and I can hardly stand on my feet.

"I will not go. I will forget her, and even if I lose her, I will not go," I decide.

I keep kneeling, crumpled over like an old bag, shaking and unable to calm down. I am hidden in my room, and every part of my body hurts. I can't beat myself up this time. Leah keeps ringing the bell. I can't, I just can't. Nobody understands me, and I don't understand myself. I think to myself: Do you know why?! Because I didn't deserve to come dancing with you, just as I didn't deserve to come to the Park with you, nor to the beach, nor walking with you. I didn't deserve anything.

Then I think: I do not deserve that, Leah, so stop ringing the bell!

She does not stop ringing the bell, she doesn't stop and the ringing persists. Tears flow from my face, and I don't know how to stop the crying. I don't know how to calm down. I hate this feeling. You can't live with this feeling. This feeling is torture, torture! I hit the floor. I kneel hard, like I want to make a hole in the floor and fall into it. I have been living in a hole for years anyway. I want to disappear!

Leah keeps ringing.

Why is she so persistent? Well, I'm not going to get up, I'm definitely not going to get up, and she certainly realises that by now.

My thoughts shift and I think, why does it have to be this way? I look into the mirror and scream. Every day is a struggle. I have to fight harder. I disappointed Leah so many times. Forgive me, Leah, I think. My fear destroyed me and the pain overwhelmed me. I am sorry. I will not give up, at least not today. I will try to be a little more alive while I am alive, while I still have a chance. Forgive me, I tell myself, and I cry.

I get up and wash my face. I am wearing a different shirt now because I completely wet the white one with tears. I want to look good for her. I sigh. I take a deep breath and get ready. I can't hear the bell anymore, but I'm sure Leah is still there. I leave the apartment, go downstairs, and go out the door at the entrance of the building. On the right, I see her leaning against the wall. She looks at me.

"I thought you wouldn't come," she says.

"I almost didn't," I sigh.

"But you came," she smiles at me.

"Yes," I tell her.

"Well, that's a victory," she says, and grabs my hand, "are you ready to dance, Enzo?"

"Always," I smile and we leave.

I'm excited. I almost forget everything - the tears, as if they were not there, the pain, too. I feel fine. I'm glad I came. I'm proud of myself, and I'm proud of being brave. I can't often say that.

Leah is beautiful, she is the best. She takes me to a new place, a place that has just opened in Pisa.

"It's summer, it's the season - there's going to be a lot of people, aren't there?"

"Sure."

"Unfortunately," I sigh.

"Don't you love people?" She looks at me and smiles.

"Don't you know the answer to that question?"

"No, I don't know. I know people love you, and everything else does not exist."

I am silent.

"It's not up to people, Enzo. Everyone is fine, in their own way. Don't look for the problem there because the problem is not there."

"The problem is in me, right?" I stop.

"No. There is no problem. Can you understand that? There is no problem, and if there is, then the problem is that you think there is a problem."

She caresses my face and kisses me. I kiss her back, somehow passionately, somehow differently, somehow more seriously than before.

"Enzo," she smiles at me.

"Please, please?!" I look at her scared, thinking that I did something wrong.

"You kiss really beautifully, with such emotion, such passion!"

She laughs and moves forward, pulling me along. Countless people pass by us. It is incredibly crowded in Pisa, but that really doesn't bother me like it used to. Leah is right, there is no problem, and just a while ago I didn't even want to imagine walking around and being part of all this. Everyone bothered me, and I found everything unattractive. I was completely uninterested in life around me.

The day I met Leah, everything changed. Here I am now, walking almost carefree through the streets of Pisa, breathing the air, watching the people, their bodies brushing mine as we pass in crowded places, and I can finally say that I feel what it is like to live in Pisa, what it is like to live at least a little, at least one day, which is enough for me.

"Here we are, here we are!" Leah says sounding happy.

In front of me I see a big red gate and a long

line of people queuing in front of it. I can hear loud music playing, and the atmosphere in the queue is electric. I'm a little nervous, but at the same time I'm incredibly present in the moment.

"Enzo, come on, we have to wait in line, come." We stand in line and wait.

I hear all kinds of conversations. People speak in different languages, laughing and joking, and some can barely stand on their feet. I have never been to a disco before. I feel nervous. I missed many beautiful moments in my life, moments I will never get back. Maybe I had the power to make it different, but I didn't even try. Over time, I came to terms with the fact that things would never change for me. But now I feel stronger, now I feel it's different. I feel that maybe things are really within my power, and that everything that happens to me really depends on me. It's very difficult to get to that point, even though it doesn't seem like it is. Now, as I begin to realise that the power I desperately seek, I already possess - I feel sorry for myself. I'm sorry for a lot of things. I feel sorry for many moments.

Time certainly passes and takes all of our chances with it. It cuts it like grass. Chances are disappearing, not a single day gives you the chance to live it again. Everything called life happens only today. This disco, this hustle and bustle, these people, and all this noise –all of it is my life, today. This is my chance. It is my moment. It's up to me what I do with all of this. I can decorate it with the happiest colours, or I can destroy it and cover it in grey. Now I see that from this moment on, I can make countless wonderful memories or just close my eyes and let it pass, leaving my bag of memories completely empty, desolate and uninteresting. Isn't that the saddest thing that can happen to a person?!

"Come on Enzo, let's go in!" Leah tugs at me.

"Is it our turn?!" I look at her. She laughs and gives me strength with the way she looks at me, letting me know that everything will be fine.

When you enter the disco, you can feel the energy of people dancing, enjoying themselves, and drinking alcohol. There are multicoloured lights that look like laser beams, flashing around the room. The music is loud, but really good. I go in, and I notice every little detail. I observe everything that happens around me. I'm curious because it's all new to me. I've never been to a place like this before.

"Enzo, let's go to the bar," Leah whispers in

my ear. I almost can't hear her, the music is really booming like thunder, but I suppose that is the point of a disco after all.

"Come on, we'll go over there and then we'll order a drink," she shows me, pulling me by the arm.

The bar is really big and there is a place to stand and order. There are different people around us, talking and drinking. I look at them and try to act like they do. I don't want it to be obvious that this is my first time in a place like this. I don't want everyone to see that I don't know how to behave. I don't want to embarrass Leah or make her regret coming here with me. She fits in so well, she merges into the crowd so easily. I don't know how she manages to do it, after all, wherever we go –she fits in. She is free from all worries, all frustrations and prejudices. She lives in the moment, with an incredible ease. I really envy her. I don't know how to do that, but I wish I could be like that too.

"What are we going to drink, Enzo?" she asks me.

"I don't know. Whatever you drink, I'll have that too," I say shyly.

"You don't know what you want to drink?!" she asks.

"I don't know," I shrug. She looks at me a little angry.

"You can't do that in life," she says, getting close to my ear so I can hear her. "You have to know what you want not just what you don't want. You are afraid to try something new, that's the problem. You are perfectly wrapped up in your comfort zone, and you don't want to leave it behind!"

I bow my head and say nothing. I know she's right. I know it's true and I really don't like it.

"I don't know. I really don't know what I want at the moment. I'm a little confused. I'm sorry, but I've never been in this kind of place before and I don't know what I want to drink. I really don't know how to behave," I say.

She smiles at me. We understand each other. She turns and orders something from the bartender. He hands her two glasses with a pink-red concoction in it, and she hands me one glass.

"Come on," she says aloud.

I take the glass and look at it. I don't know what it is, and I don't know how to ask her.

"Cheers Enzo, for us!" she raises her glass, and I do the same thing she does, because that's the only way I'm sure I'm not wrong. I take a sip through the straw of the concoction. It tastes really delicious. It tastes like strawberry, mixed with something else that I can't put my finger on. I take another sip. I like it, and I smile.

"Do you like it?" she asks me.

"Yes, it's really nice, I really like it."

"Do you want to know what this is and what it's called, then you can order it again someday?" she asks me, knowing that I don't know what I am drinking.

"I don't know. You'll order for me," I reply.

"Enzo, I won't always be here, and even if I am, don't you want to be able to order what you like on your own?" she looks at me a little angrily.

"I don't know, I haven't thought about it," I take another sip.

"Don't be ridiculous. This is a cocktail and it's called "strawberry mojito." They do it almost everywhere, but they don't do it well everywhere. It's important to have fresh strawberries, not just strawberry syrup, or it doesn't taste the same."

"Strawberry mojito? I've never heard of it," I say.

"Look, now you know. If you want to buy a drink you can order this cocktail. It's obvious you really like it," she smiles at me.

I take a sip of the cocktail again, and I actually can't stop. The taste is absolutely wonderful. It's not strong at all. It's mild, and quite easy to drink.

"Let's dance a little, Enzo," she says, and begins to move around me, turning around my body.

"Here?" I ask her, not letting go of my cocktail.

"Well, where if not here? We are in a disco, and in a disco there is dancing," she says and laughs.

"And the cocktail?" I ask her.

"Give me the cocktail, we'll leave it at the bar, next to mine. We'll dance a little, then we'll stop back here again, okay?"

Leah moves from one point to another very quickly. I just found security in this space, sipping my cocktail, now she wants to change something for me again. She's a little fast, and I'm quick to follow her, but I know she's not really fast at all, I'm just incredibly slow. You have to live as Leah lives. Leaving the comfort zone is the only way to success. I understand. It's only that I am a little off track and it's difficult for me to follow everything that's happening, be present, and seize all the moments that life offers me.

We leave the cocktails at the bar and go to the dance floor. Leah starts dancing, and of course, she does it really well. She moves freely and is cheerful, completely uninhibited and unbothered by her surroundings. I don't know what to do with my body. I try to copy some steps from the men I see dancing around me, but I think I fail at it. I look at everyone around me and wait for someone to start making fun of me for my horrible moves, but no one does. Everyone is having fun and laughing, wrapped up in themselves. I feel like I am the only one who looks ridiculous, just me and no one else.

I consider that the whole problem might stem from my fear, and people don't even notice that I'm ashamed of myself all the time. Maybe I just need to stop thinking about all the things that I haven't done and experience this wonderful moment. I don't know how much work it takes, or how much effort I have to put into calming my own thoughts, but I know that my whole life comes from those thoughts, and my life becomes what my thoughts are.

"Well done, Enzo, well done! You dance very well," Leah laughs as I try to find the rhythm with my body.

I somehow turn my arms, lower my legs, take some strange steps, while listening to the music, and moving as I feel my way around it. At the moment I feel good though, and I forget about everything around me. I gain minimal self-confidence and keep dancing. I close my eyes and indulge in the music.

The sound carries me, leading me somewhere, and I feel happy. My body moves with it. There is a smile on my face that can't be wiped off. I don't stop and I don't want to stop. I feel joyful and I dance to the music like I never thought I could, in all my life. At the moment it is clear to me that I should have tried to do all the things I thought I couldn't do, because I know how to dance very well. It's only a pity that I never dared to try it before.

Chapter 9

"Enzo, Enzo, wake up! Enzo, Enzo, get up!"
Leah's voice interrupts my dream and I open my
eyes. I realise I fell asleep in the living room, and
I see her sitting next to me, in my home.

"What are you doing here? How did you get
in?" I look, but I'm still sleepy, only half awake.

"I called you. I called you but you didn't
respond. Your parents let me in on their way out.
They're nice people. You look like your
mother," she pauses then continues, "yes, very
nice people, you do look a lot like your mother,
don't you think so?" She looks at me.

"I think so. I can also think many other things

when it comes to them, but it doesn't matter. My parents and I don't understand each other, but that's another topic," I say, yawning.

"Maybe you should stop trying to understand each other and just start feeling. Feelings are the easiest part of communication to understand."

"Maybe," I reply. "I know the origin of their behaviour, and I know it's a completely logical reaction to my behaviour and my silence, but the reason for my silence has always been related to the fear that if I spoke - I would not be understood. We were going on the same path all the time, but never reached the goal, and suddenly, damn it, we got tired and gave up."

"You run to get there as soon as possible, instead of deeply feeling your way to the goal, and enjoying discovering yourself. As soon as you find yourself, you will forgive yourself," she smiles at me. "You are very sweet while you sleep," she laughs and starts teasing me.

At that moment, watching her laugh sweetly, I realise that Leah and I are alone in my home. I can't control my thoughts, and I immediately think about what could happen. I hop off the bed.

"I have to go to the toilet," I almost run. I go to the toilet and start brushing my teeth. I get into the shower, without being conscious of what I'm doing. I deliberately stay in there as long as possible. I don't have the courage to lie in bed with her and be locked together in a space where anything can happen. I know she will be so upset about my avoidance tactics, and some day she will ask me to explain why I behave this way. I know she will ask me what my problem is. She will ask me why I avoid intimacy with her, and when that day comes, I don't know what I'll do or what I'll say to answer.

"Enzo, did you fall asleep in the toilet?!" she shouts at me after a while.

"I'm coming," I said, putting some cream on my face. "Here I am. Where are you?" I look in the living room, but she isn't there. "Leah, where are you?!" I call out.

"Here!" she yells at me from my room. I go to my room and find her standing there, staring at a fixed point ahead.

"What's the matter with you? " I ask her.

"Are you painting?" she asks, and points at my easel, which has been covered with a white sheet for a long time. I start to feel a bit nervous. Out of nowhere, I'm incredibly angry.

"Why are you snooping among my things, Leah?" I raise my voice.

"Enzo, why didn't you tell me you were

painting?!"

"I didn't tell you because I don't paint. I used to paint. It's been a long time," I answer, still sounding angry.

"Why did you stop?" she asks, not letting it go.

"I stopped because I didn't know how to paint anymore, okay."

"There's no such thing, Enzo."

"Well guess what, it exists, and I don't know what is difficult to believe about it existing."

"It's funny that you are given talent and you don't use it!"

"How do you know I was given talent? And? Have you seen anything I painted? No. Then how do you know? Maybe I'm the worst painter in the world, maybe I painted so horribly, that I did a service to the world by stopping!" I shout.

"I haven't seen you paint, but I'm sure you paint wonderfully. Will you show me something you painted?" she asks, trying to calm me down, and approaches me to give me a kiss.

"I have nothing to show you, everything I ever painted is ruined." I say and walk away.

"Did you destroy your own drawings?"

"Yes. I couldn't look at them."

"Why do you say that?"

"I thought they were disgusting, that's why."

Leah stops talking. She sits on the bed in my room and tilts her head. I try to rid myself of negative energy, but it isn't easy. I want to start a conversation, but I want a whole new conversation to happen. I want to start talking about something else entirely, I just don't know how to change the subject.

"Do you know what this is about?" she asks.

"What?" I ask.

"You can do any job, any job– and that job does not define you- but if you have talent, if you are gifted with something like that, then it defines you completely and it is a sin, the biggest sin, not to use that gift. There are people who change the world and people who see the world changing. You can change this world Enzo, I know you can. You have it in you and I don't know why you continuously run away from yourself. Don't do that, you will be sorry, you will be very sorry. One day, when it's really too late, you'll want to do it all over again, you'll want to change everything- but you can't then," she says with tears forming in her eyes.

This is the first time I see her so upset. I hurt her. It seems that I hurt her a lot.

"Leah, do you believe that a man can lose himself in himself?" I sit down next to her.

"I believe it, but I also believe you can be found again, and it can be wonderful."

I don't say anything. I look at my easel with the blank canvas propped up against it. I think about how long it's been since I even touched it. I haven't even thought about it. I left it behind like an old piece of furniture which I planned never to touch again. I see it and I feel feelings surging within me. I feel sad, I feel happy, I feel nostalgic, but I also feel a hatred that I can't even explain to myself. I manage to remember the love I once felt for painting. I manage for a moment to feel a small part of that happiness, of that euphoria, and of that incredible joy that I had in me while I had a brush in my hands. Painting was my freedom, my peace, my place in which I was most confident. I loved my little space in the world, where I painted my life with colours. Every time it was full of grey, I could change it by applying the brightest colours. I feel like a magician when I paint, and this magic was my food and my hope.

One day though, I withdrew into myself and never came out of the cave I built in my soul. I plunged into a hole and time stopped for me. I hated my paintings and my technique of painting. I hated the way the colours looked. I destroyed my little kingdom and I closed that part of my life. I feel it all again now, for the first time since that time. It feels like little pins piercing my body.

I don't know what to say and I hope Leah speaks, but she is just as quiet as I am.

"Leah, I'm sorry," I blurt out after a few minutes of silence.

"Don't apologise to me, apologise to yourself Enzo," she says.

"Alright," I say, withdrawing.

"Enough of this conversation, let's go out somewhere," she says, smiling.

"Where should we go?" I ask.

"We have no plans today, so anywhere?"

I hate to be without a plan. It's very difficult for me to function that way, but at the same time I know that not everything in life can be planned. Sometimes instead of planning, I just have to live.

"I agree," I say, and we slowly leave my apartment.

It's a nice day in Pisa so we go out for a walk. Summer seems to last forever. August is almost over, but September is expected to be even more beautiful. There are a lot of people on the streets and the restaurants are full. Leah doesn't say anything to me, I feel like she's still angry at me.

"Leah?" I say and hold her hand.

"Yes?"

"Do you love me?" I ask.

The words fall out of my mouth in a completely unplanned way. It just comes out. I really don't know why I ask her this question, but something inside me wants to know.

"Enzo, why are you asking me that?" she says.

"I don't know. I just want to know if you love me."

"Enzo, feel it, instead of asking. I think you're overwhelmed again; overwhelmed by the fear that someone doesn't love you, that you aren't good enough, and that you're doing something wrong. Why do you need to hear that people love you? Why? At the end of the day, the most important thing is for you to love yourself. You're the one who should love yourself the most."

"Yes," I say, and bow my head.

"Let's sit down somewhere. Are you hungry?" she asks changing the subject.

"Well, I'm not hungry, but we can eat something light," I say.

"Great, I know a nice little restaurant right next to the tower on Piazza del Duomo."

"Maybe," I smile at her.

We keep going, and I don't know what to think. I don't know why Leah didn't answer my question. The same thoughts spin around in my head. Leah is right. Really, why do I have to know if people love me, if they respect me, if they think of me, if they miss me? Why am I so concerned with all this? Why am I not self-sufficient? Why do I have to destroy everything with my questions and expectations? Leah opened a new horizon for me. She showed me a new point of view, teaching me to understand things differently. Leah is definitely the best thing that ever happened to me.

I see her moving carefree, how positive and calm she is, how real she is. On her face I can only see truth, only sincerity, and incredible purity. She looks effortlessly perfect. She is completely committed to life, completely present in every moment. She has incredible energy and inner strength. There is this gleam in her eyes that few people have. She truly lives and loves life. As I look at her, I feel like hugging and kissing her - but I don't dare. I pull back but can't stop admiring her.

"Here, I was thinking about this restaurant, isn't it nice?" she says, pointing to the entrance.

"Yes, it's great," I smile, as we sit down.

The restaurant is full. People sit at pretty tables with flowers in the centre of it, and there is quiet music playing in the background. The atmosphere is lovely and I feel a surge of peace flow through me. I want to be in Leah's presence. I feel good wherever she is. Leah has become my safe zone, and I am completely reliant on her.

"Leah, is that you?" I hear a woman's voice say as I look at the menu.

"Sofia! How long has it been since we last saw each other? Are you in town again? Aren't you in Barcelona?" Leah gets up and hugs the mysterious woman.

"No, I'm still there, I just came here for a week to see someone," she says.

"Sofia, I'm so glad to see you! This is Enzo," Leah points to me. I get up and say hello. Sofia's hand is wet, and I try to act like I don't notice. She seems to want to greet me with a kiss, but I avoid it because we are still strangers.

"Enzo, hello, so happy to meet you," she says.

"Me too," I say.

"Sophie, sit with us for a while," Leah says, and I can hardly believe she says that. Why would she invite a complete stranger to sit with us and spoil the wonderful time that we enjoy alone together? Why should Sofia sit with us, and how should I behave in front of Sofia?! I don't know anything about Sofia and I don't want to know. Why spend my time with a stranger who certainly has nothing smart to say?! I don't want to, I don't want to! I nod and expect Leah to notice that I'm angry. I expect her to tell Sofia to get up and leave, but that doesn't happen. Leah and Sofia are chatting, talking, laughing, and I am sitting on the other side like an intruder and feeling miserable. Leah tells Sofia that we went to the disco and had a wonderful time, and Sofia says that she heard about that place, and that she wants to go there while she is in Pisa.

"Did you like the disco?" Sofia asks me. She probably asks me just to include me in the conversation, so that I don't feel so neglected and left out. She is probably not interested in my answer at all.

"Yes," I say bluntly, expecting her to feel the anger in my voice.

Leah gives me a scolding look. I don't react because I don't feel guilty. Leah is the one who invited Sofia to our table without asking me and ended up making me feel bad and very lonely. I start sweating and feel incredibly nervous. I can't hide it any longer, so I start kicking my feet into the air aimlessly. The atmosphere at the table slowly becomes uncomfortable. Sofia looks at me, and finally begins to notice that I don't like her sitting with us. She apologises and says she has to leave, but says she wants to hear from Leah again while she is in town. She extends her hand to me and tells me she is extremely glad she met me. I shake her hand, smile, and say nothing. I'm still incredibly angry.

"Enzo, what was that about?" Leah yells at me as I look at the menu again, trying to hide the joy of Sofia's departure.

"What did I do, I don't understand?!" I pretend that I don't know what she's talking about and that I don't know what's happening.

"Enzo, you know very well you chased Sofia away from the table. Why did you behave so rudely?" she said in a raised tone.

"I don't know, was I rude? I think her sitting at the table was rude and inviting a stranger to our table without consulting me is also rude."

"Enzo, the world is not your private hole to creep into to live, do you understand?! There are people, wonderful people you will never meet if you persistently refuse to get out of there!"

"Leah, I just want to be alone with you!"

"This is exactly what I wanted to talk to you about in the park!" she says, and I listen intently. "No, do you hear me!? You want to be where there is no risk; you want to sit with people you know very well, and with whom you are safe! You don't want new things; you don't want to experience this world; you don't want to get to know it; you don't want to discover something different! You are locked in that hole of yours, and your life passes you by, your time passes you by Enzo!" she says nervously.

"Leah, it's not like that, I don't want to get involved in something that I know in advance I won't like. What's wrong with that?"

"Enzo, it's wrong that you refuse to grow, you stay at the same point and refuse to evolve! You don't fight, you don't try! I know; I know you carry pain and wounds. I know you have frustrations and scars, but you know what?! I do too! So I try, I don't give up! I try to live this life fully, I grab every moment and I live it!"

"I just want to survive, Leah," I say, and tears stream down my face.

"Life is not given to you to survive my Enzo, you have to live. If you plan to survive, you better die, because you are a corpse anyway, who only appears to be alive."

As much as her words hurt me, I know she tells me the truth, and as much as I refuse to agree with her, I know she's right. This is not the first time I behave this way, I've been doing the same thing almost my whole life. My reactions and actions have a motive, but that doesn't matter here. I know I have a choice, but at the same time it's so difficult. It often seems to me that the choice is not fair. The fight I have to fight with myself can only be won if I am persistent if I have a real desire to win and if I strongly believe. The problem is that I'm a completely different person. I've never been persistent, and I haven't had desires for a long time. I feel indifferent to almost everything around me. I've lost faith in life and in myself. I think I'll never be able to find it again. At times, since meeting Leah, pictures come back to me and parts of myself come back to me. At times, it's as if I can feel some strength and some hope, but it doesn't last long.

"Leah, can I tell you something?" I say.

"You're here."

"I know you think there are people who are changing the world, and people who are watching the world change. I also know that you think I can change this world, but I want you to know that you have changed mine. My world, small, and wrapped in grey, easily fragile, full of all kinds of pain, frustrations, and wounds, completely uninteresting, and incredibly monotonous- you changed it and made it more beautiful."

She looks at me as if she doesn't see me at all. She turns her head to the other side.

"I don't know how someone like me can change your prejudiced world, Enzo," she says angrily.

I look around and in a flash I realise that I am once again missing a moment in which I could be happy, but am choosing not to be. I can't describe how sorry I am every time I do this. I hate it in myself. I hate that trait, and I hate that need to destroy what can be good. I see Leah in front of me, the person who awoke spring in my infinitely long and icy winter. I see her grieving because I managed to hurt her too. I managed to hurt the best thing that ever happened to me. I want to tell her something, I have to speak up. This must not remain like this, my soul, no matter how empty, is still not bad and evil does not flow through my veins. I am not an evil person.

"Leah, please listen to me a little," I begin.

"I don't want to Enzo. I don't want to. It hurts me, and it doesn't hurt me for me, it hurts me for you, and for the life you've decided to live. It hurts because I'm sorry. I feel sorry, I feel so sorry that it's like this."

I don't know what to say, and I want to say everything, but I can't speak the words.

"Leah, I'm behaving like that because I'm scared. I'm scared of people, of life, of what can happen. Leah, this is how I protect myself, I'm full of anger and prejudice because I'm an incredibly sad person. I don't do it on purpose. I didn't choose it, it happened to me. Do you understand me, Leah?!" I tremble as I speak.

She looks at me and almost doesn't blink. All I see are her beautiful eyes. She looks at me scared.

"Enzo, what happened to you? Tell me. I knew from the first moment that you are different, but this anger and these frustrations come from somewhere, there must be a reason for your behaviour. It can't be accidental. What are you afraid of? Why are you constantly scared? Explain it to me," she insists, touching my hand.

I look at her and try to stay in the same place. I try not to shake my jaw, not to lose the feeling in my legs, not to break into a cold sweat, and not to feel like someone is throwing me back into an abyss from which I can't come back. In that abyss, I live too long. That black hole turned into my home.

. . .

"I don't know what to say. There are good and bad days."

"Something is happening to him, isn't it? Doctor, do you think that what is happening means that there is a chance for some improvement?"

"I hope, Mr. Moretti, I really hope. You know everything is unpredictable, and nothing is absolutely certain. It is the beauty, if I may call it that, of such cases, but at the same time the dark side of it. We've been keeping him here for the last two years because of that."

"Yes, it was unbearable at home."

"Home care was not enough, even with our help. He lost orientation completely. It was dangerous for him."

"Yes, doctor, yes ..."

"You see, we have a right to hope for the best, but we also need to prepare for the worst."

"He hasn't broken down for a long time. He hasn't had such a reaction in a long time."

"Yes, Mrs. Moretti, it's been a long time. He was talking about a woman, a woman who is to blame for everything. He blamed her, cursed her through tears, saying she destroyed everything."

"I don't know, maybe it's just a phase. We don't know if what he says means anything, we don't even know if any of it actually happened. I mean, he can say anything, can't he?"

"Yes, ma'am, but don't underestimate the truth of his words. We see a jigsaw puzzle here, and all the pieces interconnect."

"I don't know what to say anymore. I don't know, nor does my husband. We're speechless. We don't understand, we simply can't understand. We just want him to get well, Doctor. Please tell us if he will get well?"

"I can't answer that question for you. I can only tell you that what I see in him is more and more of a struggle."

"Do you mean a fight, Doctor?"

"I mean the most difficult of fights; fighting with yourself."

Chapter 10

I slept like a baby. I feel like I'm waking up from a long, winter's sleep. The sun makes me open my eyes, softly tickling my face. I get up and I feel rested. I feel like a stone fell from my heart, or like I was carrying a whole bag full of bricks inside me and I finally managed to throw it away. I have a smile on my face and I don't know why.

I get up and immediately start tidying up. There is no one home. I think of Leah and my smile immediately widens. Today I want to do something nice for her. I think maybe today I'll finally lead for a change, and suggest what we do and where we go. She'll be incredibly surprised because she doesn't think I will ever take control. I have an idea to take her to a place I haven't been to in years. It was my favourite place in Pisa.

Leah doesn't suspect anything, so it'll be a real surprise for her. I'm almost done with the arrangements, and I know she'll be down in ten minutes. She most likely expects me to leave the decision on where we will go and what we will do to her, as always, but this time I have a plan. I've even surprised myself, as I never thought I'd do this. The plans involve the palace, Palazzo Blu. I've been seriously in love with this place since I discovered it.

The palace, which is a complex of several buildings, covers an area of about 4,000 square metres and has existed since the eleventh century. It was owned throughout history by the most powerful families in Pisa. Over the years it has been damaged and been rebuilt and modified.

Today, the complex is home to the Museum of Art and Culture and has been completely remodelled in appearance, while retaining the authenticity of the main building. The museum exhibits archaeological objects and furniture, sculptures, medals, and paintings from the fourteenth to the twentieth century. The museum often hosts individual exhibitions, and exhibitions from around the world, including modern art exhibitions. I of course have a great love of painting and art in general, so I adore this place.

It opened when I was about twenty, and since then I went almost every week. I enjoyed watching, observing, and drinking in the art and culture between its walls. The inspiration, like pure water, cleansed me of all toxins, and I would pour it into my canvas through colour. It was my only peace and my only peaceful place.

Art was the only thing that managed to stop my mind and open my heart. It felt like something was taken away from me and my little kingdom seemed to collapse. I lost love, desire, and strength for everything that managed to make me happy, among all the other greys in my life. I threw art somewhere far away forever, buried it and never mentioned it again. But today is a strange day. I don't know what I think about all of this. I don't know how to go back, think of the time when I was happy, and share it all with Leah. It looks like she really was right. Our souls and our bodies always remember the time we were happy, and we can always go back to that point if we really want to.

"Here I am," Leah says, standing at the front of my favourite building.

She is beautiful as always, dressed in a sky-blue dress with small, white polka dots on it. She laughs, she sees me like no one has ever seen me before.

She sees me as worthwhile and as special. I smile at her too, and we say much more with our smiles than some people do with words. At that moment, I think about the little things in life and how often people think they are not important at all. In fact, small things are the things that break big things; small cracks can destroy the whole picture; small wounds are the ones that man can hardly stand because he doesn't expect them. Small things make a big difference. A nice word and a smile are enough to start. I know I desperately needed them, exactly when I least found them.

"Leah?" I approach her.

"Yes?" she smiles and kisses me.

"Today I want to take you somewhere; to one of my favourite places," my voice trembles as I speak.

"Yes?" she looks at me in surprise.

"Yes. I haven't been there for a long time and I honestly thought I would never go again, but today I got a strange desire in me. I want to take you there."

"That sounds great. Where? Which place, Enzo?"

"The Palazzo Blu, the Museum of Art and Culture, you know it?"

"I know it. I haven't been there and I've wanted to go many times," she smiles. "Enzo, I am so happy this is happening. I am so happy that you want to share something like this with me, something so intimate and wonderful. Do you know how proud I am of you?"

"I don't know Leah. I don't know where this power in me comes from, but I feel some desire, some euphoria, some joy, some power," I say, trembling again.

"Enzo, that means you're alive. That's how you should feel every day. You should always carry such joy in yourself, no matter what is happening around you and no matter what already happened to you."

"Yes," I bow my head.

"Maybe one day you'll want to paint again," she strokes my face.

"Leah, don't. Please don't," I tell her.

"No, I don't want to make you do something you don't want to do, but I want to say that maybe one day, when you least expect it, you'll wake up and want to paint again. You just get up and start painting. You'll paint something that you've been hiding in yourself for a long time. You'll paint yourself, on the other side of life. You'll paint your soul."

I hug her.

"Let's go, okay?" I hold her hand.

She is beautiful and I can't stop looking at her. Her face is like an angel, but she is real from head to toe, infinitely present in every second. Not everyone can do that, I'm sure not everyone can do that.

We go to the museum and the day in Pisa is wonderful, really wonderful. September is slowly chasing away the summer heat, but precisely because the temperatures will drop slightly, there will be tourists in Pisa in the coming months.

"Leah, do you want to buy us ice-cream?" I suggest, and she looks at me strangely. She laughs at me, and I laugh at her even more, because I know what's funny to her.

"Is it funny to you because it's weird for you to see me take the initiative?" I ask.

"Yes, but I'm not surprised. I'm happy that you started to say what you want, sharing things, even the simplest things. I'm incredibly happy that you're starting to function with more strength. I want you to be like that, always. I want you to be full of ideas, not to hide your magic in yourself, but to be proud of it. I want you to be confident in yourself and to be aware of how much you're worth," she says, as I notice an ice-cream shop.

"Here, I can take it from here. What flavour do you want?" I ask.

"Choose for me, I'll wait for you here," she smiles.

I go into the ice-cream shop and see a big selection of flavours on display. I'm a little confused. I panic a bit because of my fear and my passivity, but I manage to focus somehow. I'm not in a hurry, and I give myself time. I decide to consider every flavour slowly, and to make a decision based on my own thoughts. I forget the fear of making a mistake. I forget the fear that I may regret my decision. I forget everything.

"It's a damn ice cream, Enzo," I whisper, "choose something!"

I walk my eyes through the selection

carefully, and allow my intuition to guide me.

"One bacio please, and one pistachio too," I say.

"Right away," the girl behind the counter says, and smiles politely.

I buy the ice cream and take it to Leah.

"The bacio is for me, and the pistachio is for you, okay?" I ask like I'm saying it.

"Great, pistachio is one of my favourite flavours," she says and takes a lick of the ice-cream.

"Really; well, what do you know!?"

"Yes. Do you see that you know more than you think?" she laughs and slowly moves forward.

I feel good and this adds to my self-confidence. I feel that my intuition isn't new, but that it somehow comes back to me. I feel that it was here all the time, but I simply ignored it.

I walk further with Leah, and we move into the museum. We pass through many alleys. There are people all around us. We look in shop windows, comment on the things we like, and the things we don't like at all. We giggle and giggle carelessly. Quite unexpectedly, I see Leah stare at a store window. She stops, and fixes her eyes on a particular spot.

"Enzo, the shoes, look at the shoes!" she says, excitedly, holding my hand and squeezing hard.

I look in the shop window and see the perfect pair of shoes for Leah.

"It's as if those shoes were made just for you, Leah!" I say.

"Yes, yes, they are so pretty and simple, and yet so unique. Look at the little pattern on the sides, embroidered in blue, such beautiful craftsmanship," she says, showing me.

"I agree, they are amazing, they will really suit you so much."

"Yes, Enzo, they are actually a work of art. I told you, we'd find the right pair when we stop looking for them, and look, it happened. It happened by itself," she kisses me.

"Let's go in," I tell her.

"Sure?" she looks at me, rather confused.

"Yes! I can't wait to buy you those beautiful shoes, so that you can give me your beautiful shoes," I smile and pull her by the arm. The truth was, I was so worried we were not going to find the right shoes for her, and I expected her to give me her worn shoes much earlier, but Leah was right, timing is everything and all things fall into place eventually.

We enter the store and ask the saleslady for

Leah's shoe size. She goes to check in the back, and returns with the right size.

"Try it," I tell her.

She is so excited and happy, and I feel the same but only twice as much as she does. She takes off her shoes and puts on the new pair. She stands in front of the mirror and starts spinning in a circle.

"Enzo, what do you think? Do they fit me well? Do you think they fit me?" she asks.

I don't say anything but I can't stop staring at her. She is a vision of beauty in my eyes, and words fail me.

She approaches me and whispers in my ear, "Enzo, say something. Do you think these are the shoes I was looking for?"

"Leah, absolutely," I say aloud.

She giggles and hugs me. She squeezes me tight and whispers, "Thank you."

"We'll take them," I tell the saleswoman, and Leah hands her the shoes.

The saleswoman picks it up and starts packing it in, while Leah smiles and jumps little joyful jumps. Suddenly, she looks at me like a light went on in her head.

"Enzo, I want to wear them now," she says.

"Do you want to put them on now?!" I ask,

looking at her.

"Well, yes. They speak to me. They are a part of me," she says giggling. I can't stop myself from thinking that if Leah puts on her new shoes now, she'll ruin them, but I realise this is a stupid thing to think, so I manage to ignore it, and just say nothing instead.

"Great," I say, "then pack your worn pair into the box and I'll take it, can I?" I look at the saleswoman, who, listening to our conversation, realises what she has to do.

We leave the store and continue our walk to the museum. Leah is shining in her new shoes, and I can't stop looking at her. I'm carrying the box with her worn shoes packed in it, in my hand, and it makes me feel glad somehow.

"Enzo, that's the museum, right?" she says.

"Yes, that's the museum," I reply, as if my heart stops beating with excitement. I look at her from a distance and all sorts of feelings awaken in me. For a moment, my legs seem to stop on their own, but I keep walking forward. I lose my breath, my hands sweat, I feel like I will fall to the ground, but I keep pushing forward. The smile on my face doesn't disappear. I grab Leah's hand and squeeze it hard. She looks at me and understands. She knows this is the time to say something to me, to give me the strength to move on.

"Enzo, you enjoyed coming here, didn't you?" she asks me, and slowly pulls me by the arm.

"Yes," I say, "but I'm still terrified. I tremble; I sweat; I hesitate."

"Your best memories happened here, didn't they?"

"Yes," I say indifferently, and I can barely hear her. It's as if I'm not present.

"It's so wonderful. I wish I had such a place."

"What place?" I stop and get confused.

"I wish I had a place where I could feel such happiness. It's amazing how happy it can make you to have such a refuge. You'll always have shelter, thanks to your gift."

My legs stop on their own, I stop too, and for a moment I return to the place that made me happy so many years ago. Leah is telling the truth. This place is my refuge. I feel my old skin, my clear mind, my chest full of air. I feel the blood flowing dynamically through my veins and my pulse moving every time my eyes see something. I feel alive, I feel alive. We are almost in front of the museum. Leah stands in front of me and kisses me:

"I can't wait for you to show me your shelter,

beautiful Enzo." I look at her and say nothing more. There is no need for words at this moment, we talk enough. We buy tickets and go in. There are a lot of people in the museum, but it's also not too crowded.

"Enzo, look, there is a special exhibition to commemorate fifty years since the first man stepped on the moon! Look! How interesting!" Leah exclaims.

"Yes, there are often various interesting exhibitions here. The basic rooms remain the same, but in the exhibition hall everything changes depending on the schedule."

"Yes, Yes. Wonderful, wonderful," she says, looking around.

The exhibition is really interesting. The topic is history and the journey to the moon. It deals with the first people to take that step, the difficulties they faced, the complications, interesting facts about the moon, and the plans and revolutionary steps planned for the future.

"Would you like to go to the moon?" she asks curiously.

"No," I say bluntly.

"Why? I would really like it, it must be interesting," she laughs.

"There's no gravity, I wouldn't like that. I feel

like I'm floating on the ground already."

"Enzo, you weren't on the moon and you'll probably never go. Neither you nor I will ever go. The question is not meant to be technical. You should've smiled and not taken it seriously."

"You're saying my mistake is having an opinion on life on the moon, and being prepared for these things in advance?"

"Yes. You're ready for life in advance, and you're not living life right now," she replies.

"Is this so, even today?" I look at her and laugh.

"Today is the exception to the rule. Today you surprised me, today is a new day, and in it you're a new Enzo. You know what? I wish all days could be like this day. I wish this new Enzo were you, forever," she kisses me.

I caress her long, beautiful hair and think that this new Enzo is actually the old Enzo, sunk into the abyss, overwhelmed with a million frustrations, complexes, wounds and pain. That old Enzo, from time to time will appear and surprise me too. Just when I think I should forget him and come to terms with the fact that I will never see him again, he will raise his hand and give a sign of life, and say: "Do not give up on me, please."

Moving around the museum is really wonderful. I don't know how to describe how I feel. I can't believe where I am and what's happening to me. I feel like someone has taken me back to the past. The museum smells the same. I feel the same energy. My heart beats with the same speed. I look around and all my memories come back to me.

I remember every corner, every point, every moment spent here. I remember how long I stood in front of the pictures and just looked at them. I remember how simple it was then to be happy, and how complex, complicated, almost impossible it seems now.

The people who work at the museum take visitors through the exhibitions. Leah listens carefully and wants to know more about the moon. I, for a moment, separate myself from the crowd and continue walking alone. My legs carry me, and I can't believe it. It's usually the other way around, they usually stop on their own, and I have to fight them and push them forward. I feel like I'm at home, like I'm really in my shelter, where nothing bad can happen to me.

I walk around the rooms and start remembering everything I once saw. I walk through the rooms that have been preserved in their original condition, rooms in which noble families have lived for a long time. I look at their personal belongings. I feel like I'm looking at my life again, like I'm experiencing the same experience for a second time round. I feel very strange. I stand in front of the walls on which the works of art are hung and I sink into its beauty, into that other world, a wonderful world in which there are no ghosts and all people are alive.

"He escaped," she closes my eyes with her hands and kisses me on the neck.

"Leah, do you know what I love most about you?" I ask, still looking at the picture in front of me.

"What?"

"You are not a ghost."

"What do you mean?" she says.

"You exist so much that nothing else matters," I say.

"Enzo, you find the most ghosts where there should be the least. Ghosts are underestimated. Many people don't know they are ghosts."

"That's right," I agree with her, knowing how easy it is to turn into a ghost, unconsciously.

"What is this? It's nice?" she says.

"This is a very old work. It doesn't matter

what it is, what matters is how it makes you feel. That's the beauty of art, it doesn't need to be questioned and its origin is completely irrelevant, as long as its meaning is real."

"Enzo, do you miss that?"

"What?" I look at her.

Do you miss making a difference through your work, enjoying your gift, your talent, your world? Do you miss being you? She holds my hands firmly because she knows I can collapse.

"I miss it Leah, more than anything I can miss," I start to cry, and I can't stop. "How can I not miss it? Man can do without everyone, but he cannot do without himself", I tremble, I forget where I am, and I don't care who sees me.

"I know, I know it hurts," she hugs me.

"Leah, this pain is the worst. It's the most painful. Do you know why?"

"Why?" she holds me tight in her arms.

"Because it hurts afterwards", I sink into my tears, even though I've learned to swim, I lose strength and surrender.

Ksenija Nikolova

Chapter 11

"Enzo, Enzo, are you listening to me?!…Doctor, he barely calmed down."

"I know Sister. He sleeps soundly, let him rest."

"Alright."

"I see a difference. He wants to break through. These reactions are a consequence, but this is his shipwreck. He must sink once more to come to life. He has to go through this himself. It's a damn circle he's spinning round and round in."

"Doctor, do you think it's very difficult for him?"

"It can be hard for you if you lose your job,

your partner, or a loved one; but if you lose yourself, it is more than merely difficult. You are lost, and you are separated from your body. You can't assemble yourself into one piece. It's a tunnel of sadness, despair, and disorientation."

"Scary. This is a really special case, Doctor."

"Yes, but I believe in this case. I believe in him, are you listening to me, Enzo? I believe in you. I also know that you believe in yourself. Fight Enzo, just keep fighting."

· · ·

Pisa is beautiful in September. The first half of September is already passing, and Pisa is more beautiful every day. I suppose every city is probably beautiful in its own way, if you can see the beauty. I wake up and feel weird. I feel a desire, a desire to do something different today. I get out of bed and I don't know how to cope with the energy I feel coursing inside me. The energy feels big, but it doesn't weigh on me. It's just strange because I haven't felt like this for a long time. I go to the mirror and look at my face. I shake my head, as if I am scared of what I see. I peek again. I want to see my face. I'm getting closer. I'm quite close. I can almost touch my reflection. I look at my face, eyes, skin, hair, teeth, mouth, and neck. My beard is completely neglected, it completely covers my chin, and my hair is also messy. I look carefully.

"I forgot," I say to myself. I touch my cheeks, as if they are not mine. I smile to remind myself how I laugh. I have completely forgotten, but I remember memories. I feel like I'm seeing myself for the first time, but I know myself from somewhere. I feel as if I don't know the person in the mirror, but at the same time as if I have known that person all my life. I don't run away from my image. I look at myself, and immediately I smile and say:

"How messy you are, how neglected you are! Why are you not in the habit of looking after yourself better?! I really don't know how Leah can go out with you. I don't understand." I sigh. I want to change something, after a long time I feel that I want to change something. I don't know how to do that, but I know I want something new to happen. I want to like myself, and that calls for a change. These are the thoughts I think as I look at myself.

"When a man neglects himself, he will look in the mirror and be afraid of what he has become. He will feel some guilt, as if he were given more than he knew he had, and he did nothing with it. He will feel that he could have been better, but he was not. He doesn't recognise the person in front of him, and like an ordinary flower that you see every day, he wants to bloom," I say to myself.

I have to do something and decide I will ask Leah for help. I'll ask her to give me some advice. I get dressed quickly and leave the house. Leah is waiting for me downstairs, as we agreed earlier. I can't wait to see her. I run out the door. She is standing and looking at me with those beautiful and clean blue eyes, she laughs with that bright smile, all gentle and beautiful as always. Her face soothes me every time I see her. I reach for her and stroke her dark hair, kissing her on her forehead. She looks at me with her incredibly present gaze, and I am sure at that moment that there is no other truth than the one I feel when I see her.

"Leah?" I say.

"Yes, Enzo?" she asks.

"I feel like a man today," I smile proudly.

"You are a man, Enzo. You are a man every day," she laughs, teasing me, even though I know she understands very well what I mean.

"I know, but I don't feel like this every day, I

almost don't remember the last time I felt like this."

"And?"

"And I want to go somewhere, fix my hair, and trim my beard. I want to see my face. Then I want to go somewhere and buy a nice suit in which my manhood will be expressed. And then, I want to go somewhere and have dinner."

"Yes?" she looks at me in astonishment and kisses me. "Want?"

"I want to," I squeeze her hands.

"Alright then, I know exactly where to take you," she pulls me by the arm, as only she can. "I have a lot of useful information about men, thanks to all the men I've met in my life, of course," she giggles.

I look at her and my legs go numb. I don't think it's funny.

"Do you think what you said was funny? I'm serious and I'm losing my breath."

"Yes," she continues to giggle.

"I don't think so," I say.

"Enzo, I won't do this with you today, that is, I will never do this with you again. I thought we understood each other on this matter."

"Yes, we understood each other, I understand, I understand everything. But I don't understand why you have to speak with such ease, with such carelessness, every time we talk about this topic?!"

"And how should I speak? I'm not ashamed of it, it's part of me. Everything that has happened to me in my life has made me what I am today. I am proud of all the things that make me who I am, all the things that I've done, even if you don't understand it."

"Yes," I nod my head and try not to be cynical.

"You know what, Enzo? You have a problem with the sexual act, in general. You also have a problem with the woman herself, who as a being, participates in that act. I can't understand you. Why do you see sexuality as something bad, as something that people should be ashamed of?" she asks, and her question feels like an arrow hitting me straight in my most wounded place.

"Leah, please don't talk about it now. This conversation must end," I start to get annoyed.

"Yes, every time I tell the truth, you want the conversation to end!" she continues.

"Leah, stop," I close my eyes.

"Enzo, I don't know what's happening to you! Why are we arguing?! You started this! I don't know where this problem comes from, I really don't know!"

"Leah, don't, I don't want to listen!" I put my hands to my ears.

"Enzo, Enzo!" she stands in front of me and takes my hands away from my ears. I put them over my ears again because I don't want to listen. I can't calm down, I start shaking, I start sweating, and I don't feel well. I will get lost. I know I will get lost.

"Enzo, Enzo," she grabs my hands violently. "Look at me, look at me please!" she says. I don't want to open my eyes. I'm afraid, I am too afraid.

"Enzo, open your eyes, please just open your eyes and look at me!" I gather courage and dare to open my eyes. The tears are stronger than me, I can hardly stand on my feet, and I struggle with myself. I really struggle.

"Enzo, I'm sorry, forgive me. Now is not the time, I see it is not. We are not talking about that anymore, this should not have happened. Forgive me, please. I just want you to know something." she looks at me.

"What?" I ask her.

"One day you'll have to get that out of you, and I'll be here when it happens. One day, you won't be like that anymore, it will be over. Believe me it will be so."

I bow my head and I calm down a bit.

"You're not going anywhere?" I say, half anxious, half pleading.

"I'm here, as long as you are," she hugs me. She squeezes me hard. It feels like serenity, like it keeps me invisible to myself, but does not allow me to disappear. I see her and I trust her. I believe in this moment. "Shall we go?" she asks.

"Maybe," I say calming down. I hold her hand and we leave.

"Enzo, you are handsome as you are," she says to me as we walk. She runs her fingers through my hair and laughs. "I'm going to take you to a place where they will make you even more handsome."

"I don't like myself. When I looked in the mirror today, I felt ashamed. I have let go of myself, and it's not nice. I should be ashamed."

"We all have such periods. Don't expect too much from yourself. We're all just ordinary people and we all struggle in our own way, but it's important that you start to realise that you can do more, and that you deserve so much more," she explains, as she moves, gliding like a butterfly, gently and flawlessly, as if in flight.

"Yes," I agree.

"But you also have to learn to forgive me and others. Without forgiveness, you can't move forward. Letting go of things frees up space for new things, new happenings, and new people."

"The past is part of me, Leah. It's sometimes so present, so damn present, that I think I'm still there."

"Undoubtedly, Enzo, but you're here. It's your choice, you choose to exist like you're still there, you don't want to leave, you don't want to let go of the past."

"You speak as if it were easy, as if it were all simple."

"The past has no power, Enzo. The past has nothing to do with you and it doesn't hold you. It can even make you stronger. Power is in your mind. You stick to all the things that hurt you, and then say that your pain never goes away. Your magic circle is drawn by your hand."

I stare at the people passing by and for a moment I disappear from the conversation. I am indifferent, and I feel incredible pain. I am indifferent to what hurts me. I think of the people whose hearts we break, even though I don't know them, I think deeply about them. I wonder if at least one of them feels like me, does at least one of them feel the way I do? Once I met Leah and started moving closer to people, everyone seemed to know exactly what they were doing, they knew exactly where they were going, and they knew exactly what they wanted to achieve. I feel like I miss life all the time, and everyone else lives it to the fullest. I have the impression that in this world, I am the only imbecile who sees life as a concept, seemingly simple to understand.

"Here we are, Enzo, here we are!" Leah's voice brings me back to the moment. I look in front of me and I see that we are standing in front of a beautiful barber shop. "This is the best barber shop in town. I checked. Come on, let's go. We are lucky to know the right people, otherwise it's impossible to get in without a prior appointment," she says and enters the barber shop.

Inside there are several chairs, loud music, and lots of people. There are men at work, they move their hands with tremendous speed, and it looks to me like they can make magic. They cut the customers hair and beards with such ease, as if they are doing the simplest job in the world. They are incredibly skilled, and look like real professionals.

"Stefano, did you forget me?" Leah smiles at the man behind the counter.

"Leah, my beauty!" he screams in surprise,

"How long have we not seen each other, you know?!", and he comes over to hug her.

"I know, I've been missing, but everything is beautiful, as you can see," she says, looking at me.

"Leah, who is this handsome man?" he asks, glancing my way as if I were for sale. I am uncomfortable. It seems to me that I'm blushing and will soon faint.

"Enzo, this is Stefano, the owner of the best barber shop in Pisa; no, in the world, I apologise!" Leah says.

I'm quiet. I want to say something, but I really don't know what to say. I don't know how to cope with this situation. He gives his hand in greeting, expecting mine in return.

"I am Stefano, nice to meet you," he smiles at me.

I'm still quiet.

"Enzo?!" Leah looks at me.

"I am… Enzo," I murmur, and slowly give my hand.

"Enzo, welcome to our barber shop," he continues to smile.

"It's nice to be here, it's a little cramped and chaotic, but nice," I say. Leah looks at me like I shouldn't have said what I just said, but it really is true. The barber shop is beautiful but chaotic, there are a lot of people inside, but I guess that is normal. How paradoxical this is, I am the last person who has the right to talk about what's normal. I'm very uncomfortable. I hope he'll start working soon and this stupid feeling will pass.

"Alright, Enzo, how do you want us to fix you?" he asks me, running his eyes up and down my body, from head to toe. He looks at me in great detail. Leah approaches him and whispers something in his ear. He murmurs and nods.

"Enzo, I know what I have to do. Don't you worry, you are in the hands of the best," and he shows me where to sit.

I look at Leah and she encourages me to sit down. I approach the chair slowly, with baby steps. I sit down and I sigh. Leah comes up to me, and says she will go out for a bit, and come back in half an hour.

"Will you leave me alone?!" I take her hand and don't let her go.

"Enzo, you have to learn to enjoy. This is a time to relax and enjoy. You don't need anyone, you are enough. Stop thinking and free your mind," she whispers, and kisses me on the cheek, then leaves the barber shop.

I feel uncomfortable, and I'm afraid that something will happen to me. I don't know how I will survive alone in this chair, with these unknown people around me, in this mess and chaos. I really don't know how I will survive. I sigh and I try to breathe deeply. A few people gather around me and have a conversation, but I don't listen to them.

I look in the mirror and try to stay put. I panic, look at the door, and think about jumping out of my chair and running away, but I don't want to do that because I've done that my whole life. I will stay here, I decide. I will stay in this place and I will continue to sit, even if the world collapses, I will not move.

"Are you ready, Sir?" one of the barbers asks. I smile. I'm not ready but I want to act as if I am. In fact, no one is ever ready for anything if I think about it, but somehow you have to live I guess.

They start working on me. One starts on my neglected chin, and another starts cutting my horrible hair. I look at myself in the mirror and I can no longer look at myself. I close my eyes. I will open them when it is over, I think. In the meanwhile, I fly to a meadow full of flowers. I lie down comfortably like on a bed. I turn left. I turn right. I enjoy the smell around me. I'm carefree. I'm literally carefree. I'm not worried. I'm completely free of all thoughts and I don't allow anything to distract my presence from this moment. I am rolling through the meadow. I am dirty. I am dressed in white, and I am stained green from the grass, but I don't even notice it. I indulge in beauty, I indulge in nature. My mind is completely untangled. I feel peaceful and tranquil in my soul.

Suddenly, from the other end of the meadow, Leah runs up and lies down next to me on the grass. She smiles at me and grabs my hand. We start running together through the meadow, we chase after each other like little children, but she is incredibly fast and I can't reach her. I run after her, and she runs away from me. I stumble and fall, but I get back on my feet and keep running after her. I have wounds on my legs and my arms, from falling, but it doesn't hurt at all. I smile all the time and run tirelessly.

"Hurry up, catch me!" Leah yells at me and keeps running away. "Come on, catch me, I know you can!" she laughs. I keep running, and I get closer to her. I breathe deeply and feel incredible strength. I'm getting closer, I'm getting closer. At any moment I will catch her, at any moment I will finally catch her.

I open my eyes quite a bit and peek. Then I close them again. I feel a tickling, a little scratching, pulling, pulling. I listen to conversations, laughing, and shouting. I close my eyes again. I'm going to my meadow. I lie down in my peaceful and beautiful meadow. I lie down and put my hands under my head. I look at the sky, and it is perfectly clean. The sun burns and caresses my body. I take a deep breath, and fill my chest with air several times. I feel incredibly alive, incredibly present, and incredibly happy. Leah runs toward me and lies down beside me. She holds my hand and looks at the sky.

"What do you see, Enzo?" she asks. "I see the sky, how simple and beautiful it is. The sky is here every day, and I rarely notice it. I so rarely rejoice in it, and so seldom pay attention to it. It's wonderful, and it makes me feel free," I say. She looks at me.

"You are free, Enzo. Freedom is priceless. When you are free, you can do anything.

"It's wonderful. It's the most important thing." I stroke her face. I caress her. I turn to the sun and stare at the sky again. I'm free, I'm really free. Even though I feel bound, even though I feel closed, even though I feel surrounded by a circle of fire, perhaps the only truth is that I am still free.

"What a change, how handsome you are, bravo, bravo!" a voice brings me back to the little barber shop, and I open my eyes and dare to look in the mirror. I see myself.

"Who is this?" I think aloud, touching my face and hair with my hands.

"This is you Sir, only a more handsome version! Do you like it?!" the other barber asks me, and the other cannot stop clapping his hands and rejoicing.

I'm quiet as I look at myself. I don't recognise the person in the mirror, and I need time to understand what's happening. I see Leah come in through the door.

"Enzo, how wonderful you look, bravo, bravo guys, really!" she runs up to me and hugs me. "He is always handsome, but now he is even more handsome. What tidy hair, there is no neglected beard, bravo, bravo guys!" She looks at me and asks, "You like it?"

I am laughing. I really don't recognise myself. I can't say if I'm handsome, but I can say that I am really average. I look like a man, an average person who knows what he does with life. I even think that I look like a serious gentleman, very stable, very satisfied, and completely confident in himself. I look like someone who has a wonderful family and a great job. In this barber shop, everyone tells me that I have been a gentleman since I came, and while I look at myself in the mirror, I feel the same way. If there is a best version of me, then I'm currently looking at that version in the mirror.

"I like it very much, thank you. I like it so much that I think this is not me," I tell the barbers.

"Bravo, wonderful, wonderful," Stefano exclaims from the desk. For this result, it's on the house. Bravo!"

I feel like everyone is looking at me, and it's awkward but somehow nice. I like myself as I look at my face. It is a feeling that I don't feel often. It's a feeling I have not felt in a long time.

"Shall we go?" Leah takes me by the hand. "Bye boys; Stefano, I kiss you and I thank you; see you," she greets everyone in the barber shop, we leave, and we keep going.

"Now?" I say.

"I can't stop looking at you, how wonderful you are. You look really great, Enzo, really," she kisses me.

"Thank you," I say, and she laughs. "No, really, thank you for coming with me, for bringing me here, for encouraging me to do this. It means a lot to me," I kiss her as I talk.

"Enzo, I did nothing. Today you wanted to do something for yourself and you did it. Do you see how simple it is? Isn't it wonderful to do something for yourself, to look in the mirror and like yourself? It's very important for a person to be happy with himself, to work on himself, to love himself, and to be well groomed, Enzo."

I look her in the eyes, blue, penetrating, and beautiful. I caress her soft hair.

"Now is the time for a new suit," she says.

"Yes, but I don't know. I want to dress nicely," I say shyly.

"I'll take you to the right place," she continues.

"Leah?!" I stop.

"Come on, we don't have time for silly questions. See how wonderful this day is, and we have so much to do."

She pulls me by the arm, as if I were a small child dragging my mother to the nearest toy store, begging for a new toy. I don't know when last I wore a suit, to be honest. My father loves dress suits and wears them very often. He has a large selection of them and is always well-groomed. Everyone who knows him says he is one of the most fashionable and best dressed men in Pisa. Paradoxically, I didn't inherit that gene from him. He will often say to me:

"Enzo, it's as if you are not my son, it's as if you have nothing of me in you," and I don't, it's true.

I have nothing of him in me. I haven't inherited his style of dress, nor his strength and toughness, nor his cold-bloodedness. But today I feel like a stylish man. I have a desire to dress in a nice suit, and with my tidy hair and neat beard, I want to look in the mirror and like myself. I want to walk through the streets of Pisa for passers-by to see me and think that I really look exemplary. Maybe they will say to themselves:

"Look what a respectable young gentleman," and I'll smile, holding Leah by the hand, proudly walking beside me, as beautiful as she is. "Enzo, do you know what colour you want the suit to be?" Leah asks me as we move.

"I don't know?" I say, hugging her as we pass the passers-by.

"I wanted to know if you have any idea of what you're looking for, but obviously you don't yet."

"Is that bad? Did I say something bad?" I look at her.

"No, not at all, I just want to awaken it in you. I want to awaken your initiative, your preference, and your own choice. I want you to know what you want and what you do not want. I want you to have a clear vision for yourself, of the things you want, of the things that make you happy for the life you desire to live."

"You make me happy," I tell her and squeeze her close to me, firmly in my arms.

"Enzo, that's not the point right now," she looks at me, a little angry.

"Alright, alright, let me think," I calm her down, "for example, I think a grey suit would fit my dark complexion and my dark hair. What do you think?"

"Grey?!" she looks at me in astonishment.

"Okay, black?" I smile.

"Enzo!"

"Brown, dark brown?"

"Enzo, you're doing it again!" she shouts.

"Well, which one?!"

"You still have no opinion, you say something and you don't even know if you mean it, you're guessing again! It doesn't matter to you and you're not interested!"

She's right, and I know she's right. I said something and I don't even know if I mean it. That's not good. Time should not be wasted, time should not be wasted. We are here once and our lifespan is too short to say words if we are not sure if we mean it or not. We don't have time for it to matter to us. Leah is right again. I understand. I know why she's angry at me.

"Leah, I'm sorry, you're right. Here, I don't know what kind of suit I want, but I really want to think a little, and try to find out what colour would suit me best. Okay?"

You should feel free to think, and there is a large selection in the store, but when you see something you like, you will just know," she smiles at me. "We are very close, we will be there soon," she adds.

It's easier for me now. I start thinking as we walk. I don't even know what I would look like in a suit, but I try to picture it in front of me. I try to feel how that suit would fit my body and how it would move with me. I might try something a little classic, something simple, a timeless suit– yes, probably; or maybe I want my father to see me in the suit and want it - yes, for sure.

"What colour do I want my suit to be?" I whisper, as Leah walks up to me, but she doesn't hear me. I analyse myself to try and figure out what I want.

"Who is Enzo?" I whisper again. Enzo is a simple guy, Enzo doesn't want to experiment, I think. Enzo once wanted to paint, but that never separated him from his simplicity. Enzo's complication lies in his damn simplicity. Enzo should wear a black suit, because in such a suit he will be most comfortable," I mutter.

"Enzo, here we are, come on, we're coming in," she tells me, like a restless child, hopping into the store.

"Hello, how are you, Mr. Federico?" she says to a gentleman who looks like a true fashion connoisseur. He is well-groomed, dressed in a suit, smiling, and he hugs Leah:

"My beauty, how are you? I haven't seen you in a long time!"

"I'm good, Sir, I'm good. We haven't seen each other, but you know how much I love you, don't you?!" she says.

"Leah, you are my hot-blooded little princess!"

"Mr. Federico, this is Enzo. We're here today because Enzo wants to buy a new suit, so of course I brought him to the best place!" she laughs.

All Men Love Leah

"I'm glad, Enzo. I'm Federico. Welcome to our family shop for men's suits and shirts. We've been working here for fifty years. Everything you see is made with a lot of love and style. Whatever you choose, you won't go wrong, believe me," the gentleman laughs.

"Thank you," I say and browse the store.

It's a really beautiful place. It's clear that a lot of love and effort is invested in it. I can see that right away. The suits are beautifully displayed and there is a large selection. I hope the dust in the space doesn't damage these beautiful suits, but I'm sure they have a solution for that little problem. The gentleman sits down in his chair and Leah hugs me.

"Enzo, take a look, don't rush, Mr. Federico is here for everything you need, and you?!"I look at her. "I will leave you to enjoy this wonderful place. I'll be back in a while," she laughs, winking at Mr. Federico and leaving the store.

"Okay," I mutter, and take a deep breath.

"Enzo, I'll go back to reading, I'm reading an exceptionally good book. You go ahead and browse, feel free to ask me anything you want. We never force our customers, we let them discover themselves and find what they want for themselves. I'm here for help, so enjoy." He puts on his glasses and starts reading.

"Alright, alright," I murmur again. I start to look. It's a little hard for me to focus. There really is a great selection. There are almost too many different types of suits and shirts. I really don't know where to start and how to start at all. I sigh. I move to the left side of the store slowly, and decide to start from there.

"May I touch them?" I ask Mr. Federico.

"Well, of course Enzo if you don't touch them, you can't know if you like them. Feel free to touch, explore– explore and ask. That's how it's done," he says, continuing to read his book.

"Thank you," I say, and start looking at the first suit. I touch the material, I examine the pattern, the way it's made, the colours that are used. It's too specific, it has soft shades of orange in it, and I know it's not for me. I continue on to the next suit. I touch the material, I reconsider the way it's made, but this suit is too specific and unique for me. I want something simpler, something much simpler. I continue looking. Leah told me that when I see what I like, I will know. I hope so. I look at another suit, in brown tones, and immediately put it back in its place. It seems to me that brown is not my colour. Leah would be really proud of me if she could see how great and concise I treat the suits. I keep looking, and I come across suits with happier colours, light blue, yellowish, bright red. All the suits are stylish, but I wouldn't like those colours on my suit. I love classics, I love timelessness.

"This one!" I scream out.

In my hands I hold a black suit, impeccably made, seemingly simple, and a necessary basic. "Wonderful. Wonderful!" I say out loud.

"Yes, yes, usually that's the reaction when you see the suit that's tailor-made for you. Let me look at you," Mr. Federico looks at me from head to toe and smiles. "Alright, now I will bring your size. Come on, the changing rooms are there," he shows me politely. I enter the changing room and wait for him to bring the suit I chose.

"Take it," he hands it to me. "I also brought a shirt to give you a complete picture," he smiles at me.

I take the suit and the shirt and put them on the hanger in the changing room. I look at them and admire them. The shirt is white, clean, perfectly tailored, as if drawn. At that moment I realise that I would choose an identical shirt myself. It will fit perfectly with the suit, I think. I start to take off my funny clothes and slowly dare to touch the new things and put them on. I'm afraid of damaging them. I'm afraid of doing something to break them. They are wonderful, and I don't know if I deserve it. I put my shirt on and look in the mirror. It's perfect for me. In fact, it's as if it were tailored just for me. The gentleman really knows what to choose, he really is a professional. I close the last button and smile. I like it very much. The shirt makes me look like a serious adult, modern, and urban.

"Is everything okay?" Mr. Federico calls.

"Yes, yes," I sigh. I continue to dress, and put on the suit pants slowly, being careful not to accidentally damage it. I fasten it then I put on the upper part of the suit and fasten it too. I raise my head and look in the mirror.

"Enzo, is this you?" I whisper.

"Enzo, go out and see how you look," Mr. Federico calls out to me again.

"Coming," I step out of the changing room, and Mr. Federico looks at me as if he is seeing a ghost.

"Miracle, what a miracle!" he calls out. "Shoes, we need shoes," he says, entering a room next to the changing room. "We don't sell shoes, but here is a pair, I think they are your size, just

to see what all this would look like with shoes,"
he smiles and hands me a pair of elegant, black
shoes.

"Try them, you can't get the right impression
without shoes," he added.

I take off my sneakers and put on my shoes.
They are the right fit for me. I straighten up,
stand up tall, and approach the mirror, slowly
and shyly.

"Enzo, this is a clear hit! All the customers
leave here satisfied, but I rarely say that a suit is
tailor-made for someone. This is tailor-made for
you, you don't need any alterations. You don't
need anything! Well done, well done! Look at
yourself, go to the mirror! Look, don't be
ashamed!" Mr. Federico encourages me.

I look in the mirror and see Mr. Federico's
face behind me, pleased with what he sees. I
can't explain exactly how I feel. I look at myself,
I really don't know if this is me or someone else.
I don't know if this was me all the time and I was
just hiding, or if this is me now, some new man,
some new Enzo. I don't know and I'm confused.
I turn around and I look at myself from all
angles, I notice even the smallest details. I like
what I see, I'm proud of the image in front of me.
I close my eyes, and I feel this moment intensely.

I'm in my flower meadow again, dressed in a suit, with tidy hair and a clean face, walking. Birds are flying around me and they seem to be telling me through the song that I look good. I walk, smiling and confident. Leah appears in the meadow and she is as beautiful as ever. She doesn't recognise me. She needs to get closer to me to make sure that it really is me. I kiss her, caress her face, and she looks at me with those beautiful eyes, full of pride.

"Enzo, I can't stop looking at you! Enzo, you look beautiful!" Leah suddenly comes in through the store's front door, and runs toward me. She hugs me.

"I knew, I knew!" she says, and kisses me.

It's awkward for me, but I'm happy and I choose to focus on that. It's a beautiful moment and I want to stay here forever.

"Mr. Federico, you've done a fantastic job!" she says, and he smiles and hugs her.

"Leah, the suit is tailor-made for him, I did nothing special, believe me. It was destiny."

"And the shirt is beautiful," Leah continues, touching the shirt on my body.

"Yes, I gave it to him so he could see the full picture," Mr. Federico explains..

"We'll take this too, we must take this too.

Right, Enzo?" she looks at me with a childish smile.

I'm quiet because I don't know what to say.

"Enzo?!" she looks at me, scolding me for my silence.

"I like the shirt too, yes," it fits perfectly with the suit."

"Then, done!" Leah says joyously. "Enzo, don't change your clothes, Mr. Federico will pack your old clothes in the bag."

"Leah, but the shoes aren't mine, I'm wearing sneakers, I can't go out like this," I begin to untie the shoes.

"It's not a problem, it's not a problem, you will take them and return them to me another time. Really, I insist, take them. They are just here for decoration anyway. Don't worry, take them," suggested the kind Mr. Federico.

"Is it really ok Mr. Federico?" Leah asks. "Thank you, you're the best!" she hugs him. "You know, we're going to dinner after this. We'll return your shoes to you later, Mr. Federico."

"No problem, I'm glad you like it," he laughs, taking my clothes from the changing room to pack it in. He hands me the bag with my old clothes, and I look in the mirror, still not sure who I see in the reflection. Leah and I say goodbye to Mr. Federico and we leave the store.

"I'm uncomfortable, because I have this suit and this shirt because of you, and I don't deserve it."

"Enzo, come a little, let's go sit on a bench in the park over there." She holds my hand firmly and for a short time she sits down, while I don't know if I should sit or stand, because I'm afraid of staining the new suit.

"Leah, I don't know if this bench is clean."

"Enzo, the world isn't clean, nothing is clean. Your soul should be pure, and the rest is uncertain. Sit down!" she orders me, and I sit down and notice there are a lot of people around us, walking, sitting, and relaxing.

"Enzo, let me ask you something. You gave me a beautiful pair of shoes, didn't you?"

"Yes," I mutter.

"Why do you think I deserve those shoes?" she continues.

"Because there is nothing you don't deserve!" I answer in a raised tone.

"Alright then, so why do you think you are different from me? If I deserve everything in this world, then why do you think the same doesn't apply to you?"

I bow my head. I'm confused and I don't know what to say. I don't want to quarrel with Leah. This day is so wonderful, and I don't want to ruin it.

"Leah, it doesn't matter now," I murmur.

"It's very important, Enzo! How can you not see?" she says out loud.

"Leah, I don't know what you want to hear from me, really," I say, bowing my head again, not having the courage to look her in the eye.

"Answer the question I asked you," she says, calming me down.

She takes my hand, and puts it on her leg.

"Leah, I'm not like you, I just am not. I know you don't see it and I know that you persistently see a man in me who is talented, who is worthwhile, who is capable, who deserves everything, but I simply don't see it in myself. I feel special today, but I know it's only today, I know it's not me, I know it won't last. I know that. I'm reconciled to my truth," I explain and tremble.

"What truth?!" she asks me.

"The real truth," I tell her.

"Enzo, the truth is so abstract that you shouldn't tell it to anyone, it's enough for you to know it. Why is there truth? It exists to guide you, to give you hope, to save you. You have the right to desire the best truth for yourself and you have the right to believe in it. You mustn't reconcile with your truth if you don't like it. You need to change it."

"No one asked me if I liked my truth," I told her.

"We have no power over what others do, Enzo, but we have incredible power over ourselves, over our minds, over our behaviour, that should be your focus, Enzo," she hugs me, and I tremble.

"Leah, if you only knew ...," I mutter.

"I know, Enzo. I know everything. You don't have to say anything. You don't have to say anything at all. Let your soul speak to you, let it cry so that it calms you down," she hugs me even harder, holds me in her arms, and I feel safe.

I can't calm down, I continue to tremble. I forget that there are people around me. I don't hear the sounds anymore. I lose contact with the ground my feet touch, I feel like I'm floating through space again, and I am not present at all.

"Enzo! No, Enzo! Come back, Enzo! Where are you going?! Don't go away, please don't go away. Don't leave me, Enzo! See what a beautiful day we have, don't go away! Stay, stay with me to finish this wonderful day! Enzo, please, endure and stay!"

Leah pulls me with her words, she pulls my soul back, as if I am tied with a rope and she unties me. I have a picture in front of my eyes, but my focus is completely lost. I hold on to a hair, to a hair. Her words are like a gentle breeze which appears in the greatest heat and saves me.

In the same moment that I think I will collapse and disintegrate from the heat and the pain, her words caress me like a pleasant breeze. It caresses my face and my body, and suddenly, despite all the pain, I find some incredible strength, a strength I didn't know I had in me. At that moment, I have the courage to look again, and I have the courage to try again. I feel that force rush through my veins. The force pushes through my blood, makes it run faster across my body, and suddenly I feel the urge to live. I obviously like it, I think. I obviously live, and I laugh, and I walk, and I breathe fully again, and I see new things again. I talk and I rejoice. I obviously feel like living because I give up every time but I can never die. She is obviously fighting for me, and the gentle wind that caresses me, and her words that appear at the right time every time, are a sign that I have reason to believe. Maybe if I'm really lucky, one day I'll paint my truth again, the way I want and the way I know. After I paint it, I'll look at it and feel proud. I'll be incredibly happy because I'll see something in front of me that I like, something which I believe in immensely.

"Leah," I say softly as I raise my head, and for a moment I seem to stop floating. I look at her and I know that there is no need to tell her anything anymore. The way she looks at me, I see that she knows everything.

"Let's sit down somewhere, let's go somewhere to eat. I want this day to be exactly the way we said it would be. It's very important for me to stick to my word, and it's especially important that what I wanted to happen to me must happen, you know?" I tremble again. "Lately, I feel powerful and privileged enough to do the things I love. What a wonderful feeling it is to have strength and desire. How immensely beautiful it is when you live," I laugh.

"That's right, my dear Enzo, that's right. You're living!" she smiles. "Okay then, are we going?" she continues in her melodious voice. "It's a little early for dinner, but it's never the wrong time for the right things, is it?" she takes me by the hand and pulls me forward.

"Where are we going?" I ask her.

"I don't know, we'll see. The first place we like will be where we sit. Agreed?" she says, because she knows that spontaneity is not my strong point. When I met her, it was incomprehensible to me how spontaneous she was, and yet at the same time so organised. I don't feel like that anymore. Now I understand it because I realised that spontaneity is desirable in everyone's life.

"It's getting hot, again isn't it?" Leah says as we go for a walk.

"Yes, definitely," I say.

"We can travel somewhere," she adds, "for the weekend, somewhere in Italy. You can choose where," she says.

"Shall we travel?" I look at her confused.

"Yes, one weekend. Don't you want to?"

"Well, I've never been anywhere Leah."

"And you have no desire to change that?"

"It's not a wish. Sometimes, as much as I have a desire, I may not have the strength to fulfil that desire. Do you understand?" I look at her and feel the fear start to attack me again.

"No, I don't understand you. Explain it to me, since you are the one who knows yourself best. You don't want to travel?" she asks me incredulously, and I know she knows the answer to the question.

"I've never travelled, so I guess I don't like it."

"And how do you know you don't want to travel, when you haven't been anywhere?" she continues.

"I don't know, I just know. My parents love to travel. They've been almost everywhere."

"And you?"

"I stayed at home."

"Who did you stay with?"

"Who do you think I stayed with?"

"I don't know. Who did you stay home with while they were travelling?"

"When I was little, with the nanny; when I grew up I was left alone, because I grew up."

"Well, when you were little, you couldn't possibly know if you wanted to travel or not. They could have taken you with them without asking you. Later when you grew up; how did you know you don't want to go anywhere?" she persisted, looking sadly into my eyes.

I start shivering and breaking out in a cold sweat. The feeling of fear completely overwhelms me and I feel trapped again.

"I only knew that I didn't want to and that I

was scared. I was afraid of the unknown, and I didn't want to feel uncomfortable. When I was young, no one depended on me. When you are very young, things happen to you, they just happen to you and you have no control over it. Don't ask me any more questions about the time I had no control over, because I have no explanation for anything," I say trembling uncontrollably.

"Enzo, do you know what?" she stands in front of me.

"What?"

"I think that the time where you had no control, swallowed the time in which you should have control. I also think you don't want to get out of that time when you were out of control, and I think you're still living there," Leah says.

"I don't know what to say, I really don't want to talk about it at the moment. Maybe at some point I will be able to face everything on my own, but I can't at the moment, I just can't. We can talk about this another time, okay?" I say agreeing with her, wanting to avoid the topic and trying to talk about something else.

She looks at me in the eyes and strokes my hair.

"Alright," she says and kisses me. It calms me

down and suddenly I'm fine. She always knows how to calm me down, but she also knows how to upset me. Leah knows so much, at times I even think she's omnipotent and can do anything.

"Enzo, what do you think of this small, sweet restaurant?"

She stops in front of a restaurant that I think is lovely. It's intimate, with a beautiful little terrace. Almost everything in the restaurant is white, and there are small, lit candles on the tables, which makes the atmosphere romantic and special.

"I like it, maybe," I say and take her hand, heading to the entrance ahead of her. She looks at me questioningly. I know this is not normal for me, but today I'm wearing a dapper suit and I'm perfectly groomed, so I want to act like a real gentleman.

"Welcome," we are greeted by a polite waiter.

"A table for two, please," I say.

"Do you have a reservation?" he asks me. I look at Leah and for a moment I'm confused. She is quiet and leaves me to take charge. I want to exude confidence, so I say,

"No, we came spontaneously. We liked your restaurant and we just decided to sit here." I smile at Leah, who I know is enormously proud of me at the moment.

"Great, Sir. Welcome," the waiter replies, pointing to a beautiful table in the corner of the restaurant. We sit down, and he brings us a menu. I can't take the smile off my face.

"What's funny, Enzo?" Leah asks me, opening the menu.

"Did you hear him?" I ask excitedly.

"What?"

"He called me sir," I smile.

"Of course, you are a gentleman. I don't know why you would think you are not. There is nothing strange here," she says.

"I know, it's the getup and the hairstyle – and the horrible beard I no longer have, of course, but it feels good anyway," I smile again.

"Enzo, it's not about that at all. Those things are just a plus, but can't perform the wonders that you think they can. What we are comes from within us, from our soul. The clothes and the style only accentuate what we already have, do you understand me?" she looks at me, touching my hand.

"I understand, but still, I only feel like a gentleman today. It must be something," I bow my head.

"It's up to you," she says, "you need to feel

that way every day."

I sigh. I'm not saying anything more, I know Leah is right. Leah is always right and she does it in a weird way. I don't know how to explain it, but I look at her and my entire body tingles with excitement and happiness.

"I want to dress like this more often," I tell her.

"Get dressed, no one is stopping you," she says and smiles.

"Yes, no one is stopping me," I smile, "except me."

"What are we going to eat?" she asks.

"Pasta with pesto sauce, bruschetta with tomato and mozzarella, and we can drink from their homemade white wine," I surprise her with my confidence again, and she throws the menu down on the table in excitement, and starts applauding. Everyone in the restaurant looks at our table, but that doesn't matter to me at all. I don't know why, but I don't care about other people's views at the moment. I just focus on what is happening to me. I can hardly believe I am being this way, but I really am.

"Thank you, this applause is well deserved," I smile.

The waiter comes and I order for both of us. He brings homemade white wine to our table and

I make a toast to the wonderful day. Leah is staring at something in the distance, but I can't see what, she doesn't even see me holding the glass in front of her. There's a sad look on her face.

"Leah, are you okay?" I ask anxiously. "Let's make a toast, to us, to this wonderful day." She lifts her glass, and looks at me.

"Cheers, Enzo, to you!" She drinks from the glass a little, and looks away again.

"Leah, what's wrong with you? Are you sad?" I ask her.

"No, Enzo, on the contrary. I'm happy," she says, and sighs softly.

"I'm happy too, but why do you seem sad to me?" I continue.

"I'm happy because I know that very soon you will be great, and that happiness saddens me a little bit as well," she says.

I look at her and I really don't know what to say. Maybe I shouldn't say anything because I really don't want to say something I don't mean. After all, that's another thing I learned from the beautiful Leah, I know that life is really too short to say words we don't mean.

The bruschetta arrives and it looks wonderful. Leah cheers up immediately, and it calms me down. The food is so good, and the wine is incredible. My thoughts are far away but I'm present in the moment. I'm so present that I'm sure of every little detail around me.

I know that today is Wednesday; I know that we said goodbye to August; I know that September is wonderful. I know that my hair is tidy and I don't have a horrible beard; I know that I'm wearing a suit I liked from the first moment I saw it; I know I'm sure I like the way I look; I know we are sitting in a wonderful restaurant in the heart of Pisa; I know we are eating delicious food and drinking nice wine; I know there is nice quiet music playing in the background; I know that the candle on the table emphasises the sparks in Leah's blue eyes; I know that Leah is sitting on the other side of me and I can see her clearly; I know that this moment completely carries me; I know I have the right to my wonderful truth, and I know this is all mine.

Chapter 12

Today the sun loves me very much. It caresses my face like never before. I wake up and smile automatically. I always thought that to smile, you have to have a specific reason, but today I laugh just because. I just feel good. I feel like I was a broken jigsaw puzzle with pieces scattered everywhere, and now those pieces are back together, making me whole. I feel like I am my own. I am in touch with every part of myself, completely. I don't know how this happened, but

I don't want to ruin the wonderful feeling with a million questions.

I no longer want to live with the constant questions and fret over answers I can't find. I did this to myself just to feel unhappy, to feel justified for staying stuck in a shell. The shell was supposedly a safe place, but nothing happens in the shell. There is no news, no progress, no hope, and no faith in the shell.

Painting used to be my wonderful refuge. I created my own world through my art, and it opened me up to other worlds. In that world I didn't hide and I didn't stand still in one place. I was constantly growing. I was full of imagination and desire. I turned into a better and happier person, thanks to the power of art. In that world of mine, time passed faster than usual, because I was constantly doing something and progressing with each passing second.

In my shell, I am far from the storm, and I am far from the cold, but yet I turn to ice. Nothing from the outside can hurt me, but I am wounded deep within my soul, and I wither. I have no contact with the outside world. I am in complete isolation and withdrawal, until the moment I decide I want to change something, like I decide today. Today I have different thoughts and a different energy that moves me. Today I feel so calm that I think of breaking my shell forever. I feel like crushing it from the ground and tearing it to pieces, just as the pieces of my puzzle were scattered everywhere, leaving me without a picture.

Today is Friday and Leah and I are leaving. She suggested we go somewhere for the weekend and we decided to go to Florence. Leah has been to Florence several times and she told me how beautiful it is. I've seen pictures of Florence and I've heard of the city and its majesty, but I've never visited it. My parents went to Florence often and always came back with good reviews. Many consider Florence to be the most beautiful city in Italy. It is crowded with tourists though, and is a constant destination for people visiting Italy, partly because of its beautiful architecture.

I'm getting ready for the trip and I'm very excited. I can't believe I'm going to travel. I feel like I'm living in a dream, in a wonderful dream. I have to admit that I'm proud of myself, because lately I've been able to move forward and look backwards less and less. I manage to believe and to hope. Every day I progress, and every day I feel better than I did the day before. I don't know exactly what happiness is, I wouldn't know how to describe it, but I know that I feel it right now.

I don't know what to bring with me, not really, not at all. I have some anxiety about travelling, but Leah organised the whole trip. She told me that all I had to do was pack my bag and get rid of negative thoughts and questions.

"We're going to have a good time, please don't think, please try to experience this trip as something new and wonderful," she says.

I know it's true and I really want to experience this journey that way. I don't want to be worried at all, and even though I am a little scared, I'll do my best not to focus on it. I don't want to allow the fear to possess me completely. I missed a lot of things in life because I felt scared, and I don't want to do it anymore. I indulge in life for the first time. I don't want to protect myself anymore. If something needs to happen to me, let it happen to me. I know that the worst things happen anyway, even when you think you are the most protected. Fear is paradoxical in every sense of the word, and instead of being afraid of it, I want to get to know it again, hoping to realise how much I overestimated it.

I look at the bag in front of me and carelessly throw a few pieces of clothing in it. I haven't been so worried about small things for a long time. I'm going to Florence, that's all that matters. Leah told me that when you travel, the most important thing is the energy you carry with you, and if it isn't pure and positive, you will never have a good time. I strongly believe in that, that's why I don't care about unimportant things.

I take a deep breath before closing my bag, and look out of the window in my room. It was never clearer to me than now; life is happening outside of my room. Life happens every day; life has to be lived. Today I feel like I'm living my life. I even think that if someone looked at me from the outside, he would say:

"Look at that guy, he really lives his life. He does so many different things, and he doesn't squander his time. He fulfils his desires. Just look at him, I envy his energy."

The doorbell rings and I get ready to go. Leah is waiting for me at the front of the building.. She is wearing a big, light pink hat, with a long, white linen dress. She looks like she stepped out of a fairy tale.

"You are incredibly beautiful Leah. You are incredibly beautiful," I kiss her.

"We're going to Florence, nothing else

matters," she laughs.

"I dressed very casually, I wanted to be comfortable," I say feeling shy, and as I say it I look down at my outfit and my shoes.

"Enzo, when you wore the suit I told you that the clothes do nothing special. Everything comes from within. It's important how you feel," she strokes my face.

"I feel excited and lucky," I tell her.

"I can see you do, it's obvious. Happiness is always visible, you can't hide it, even under the most elaborate clothing."

I smile and kiss her again. She's wonderful, I think to myself as we make our way to the train station.

"Are we going? We just have to hurry a little bit to catch the train." I walk after her, carrying my bag in one hand, not believing that I'm actually on my way.

"When does our train leave, Leah?" I ask her curiously, as if I ride a train every day. I don't know why I have a habit of asking so many questions. I think by asking questions, I get a sense of control, and at the same time I think that I'm neutralising my fear. I've never tried to simply experience what will happen to me. Today though, I'll try. I'll do my best, and I won't repeat what destroys me.

"Maybe today is the beginning of your new life, Enzo," I mutter to myself and walk towards Leah.

"The train leaves in ten minutes, Enzo," she says, hurrying.

"Will we make it?" I look at her anxiously.

"Of course, and if we don't get there, there's always another train, right?"

"Well, yes," I smile uncertainly. "How long will the trip take?" I continue with the questions.

"About an hour," she replies.

"Alright, alright," I mutter, trying to catch up with Leah.

"We should've left earlier," I say.

"Enzo!" she stands in front of me. "Are you panicking? What's wrong with you?"

Leah knows me, she knows me well. She knows exactly what to say to me.

"Yes, I feel incredibly panicked. I haven't been anywhere, I've never travelled. I haven't changed my surroundings, and I haven't faced the unknown. I'm afraid, Leah. I'm nervous. I don't really know how to behave. I was sure today would be a great day, but it's overwhelming me. It beats me, panic beats me! "I start to tremble and sweat. Not all people are the same Leah, they are just not! Why is it so hard for you to understand that? Why do you always expect something from me? I feel like I'm disappointing you, I feel like I'm not good enough, and I'm not, look at me. I'm scared again. I want to shut myself in my stupid shell again. I want to avoid life again Leah. If I avoid it unconsciously, it just passes," I say out loud.

"Enzo, I don't expect anything from you. You don't understand, you don't understand the point of all this. I never expected you to be someone else, I just wanted you to be a little more you, because I know you are wonderful, you are magical, you are special. I see who you are. I know what you are like. I don't need someone else Enzo, I need you. You don't want to go out, you don't want to show yourself, you don't want to meet yourself. How do you know what Enzo can handle? You don't give Enzo a chance, you don't challenge Enzo. You're judging Enzo, and you don't even know him. You don't know each other, do you understand?" she hugs me.

We stand by the noisy roadside, and there are countless people passing by us. Leah and I hug, we flee into our world. She doesn't let go of me, and I hold onto her tight. I begin to feel calm and peaceful. Leah is right. I know she's right, and

I've never doubted her words, but I can't stop feeling everything I feel. I have good days and bad days. I have good and bad moments, and I turn around like this in a circle. I was sure that today would be a great day. I was sure that today I would not stop once and run out of air, or feel lost and scared, like the ground under my feet is falling away. I'm not as strong as I thought. I'm not as grown up as I think.

"Enzo, we're going on a trip now. This is something new for you. You've never travelled in your life. It's quite understandable to be afraid, to feel nervous, and to experience some panic, but why do you allow that to ruin this wonderful day? Listen to me, you'll be fine. Whatever happens, you'll survive. It's human nature to want to survive, so believe me, when you come from that moment of loss, even if you get lost, you'll get back to where you were. You will become stronger and you'll continue to grow, and one day, you'll win," she kisses me and squeezes my sweating hands.

I take a deep breath and close my eyes. I clear my thoughts and try to be brave. I want to be strong. I want to win.

"Shall we go?" I say, and she smiles at me.

"We are going. We missed the train, but as I

told you, there is always a next one," she laughs out loud. She speeds up her steps, and I try to follow her as we move through people, cross streets, pay attention to cars, and for a moment I feel that I'm part of everyday life again. Leah goes too fast, I can't reach her.

"Leah, you're in a hurry," I can barely speak.

"Go forward. Go ahead. If it hurts, go faster," she says.

Chapter 13

We're on the train to Florence and Leah is sitting by the window. I'm right next to her. There is a couple sitting opposite us, old enough to be somebody's grandmother and grandfather. The grandmother rests her head on the grandpa's shoulder and almost falls asleep. He reads a book with his big framed spectacles resting on the bridge of his nose. How beautiful this picture is, I think. I imagine they have been together for a long time.

Perhaps they've known each other since their young days and fell madly in love with each other right at the beginning. Maybe they had fun for a while, then got married, and a short while later the grandmother gave birth to a child, and then soon after that, another child. Their family was the most important thing to them; they had lunch together every Saturday, and took regular walks on Sundays. The children grew up in a loving and happy home, everything was discussed openly in the family, and the children could rely on their parents when problems arose, without question. After the children grew up, got educated, and started working, they became independent and went on to fulfil their dreams. As parents, they were always available to their children, yet at the same time, incredibly proud of their independence.

Now in their adult years, the grandparents decided to dedicate their time to travel and research. Together they choose destinations they've never visited before, and travel often. They walk as much as they can, drink coffee, eat good food, and enjoy the life they've built together for so long. They talk about the happiness they have, and every time the grandmother feels sad, the grandfather knows how to cheer her up. They are still in love with each other after all these years, but at the same time they are best friends.

At one point I realise that I've been staring at them for a long time, and that it's a little uncomfortable. I look away. I look at Leah. She is asleep and leaning her head against the window. She sleeps peacefully, like a baby. I hug her and gently lean her head on my shoulder. I love her and feel safe with her next to me, like the grandmother and the grandfather feel beside each other.

"Enzo, have we arrived?" she wakes up.

"No, not yet," I tell her.

"I fell asleep," she smiles. "What were you doing?"

"I saw beauty."

"Yes?" she looks at me in astonishment.

"Yes," I answer.

"And did you learn something new from that beauty?"

"I learned that life is very simple, in principle," I laugh.

"But you enjoy complicating it, don't you?"

"I wouldn't say that I'm complicating my life. Well, I'm not the only one complicating my life."

"Sure," she confirms with her head, "but you're the one who allows it in the end. You allow it, and you somehow continue it," she pinches my hand.

"I really don't want to talk to you about this, especially not on a train," I laugh out loud.

"Look, that's progress," she begins to clap her hands in applause.

"What is progress?" I look at her in astonishment. I completely forget that there are people around us and that we may seem strange, but maybe that's the progress Leah is talking about.

"The joke is progress; to joke about your own pain and for a moment to forget that the pain is pain. It's progress, do you understand?" she smiles at me.

I lower my gaze and say nothing. It's nice to hear Leah say that. I feel a little proud of myself.

"You're on the right track, my dear Enzo. You've moved forward, that's for sure. Now you mustn't stop. Don't even think of stopping," she sighs and turns to the window. She seems sad to me again. I don't know why she's sad again when she tells me how I'm progressing. I never want to lose Leah. No matter where I am, no matter how I feel, or what I do, Leah will always be here. I caress her hair. I'm sinking into the moment. How beautiful she is, she knows me best, she knows my soul, my mind, my thought.

She will always be a part of me, I'm sure of that.

"Santa Maria Novella, Santa Maria Novella," is announced on the train.

"We've arrived Enzo!" Leah says excitedly, and immediately her mood changes. The train stops, and we get out. There are a lot of people at the station and everyone is rushing somewhere. Everyone is waiting their turn.

"Enzo, look out for the bag. Follow me, let's get out slowly," Leah says, and steps forward. There are really too many people as we get out.

"Enzo, the hotel is not very far from here, a kilometre and a half, about," Leah says. "You want us to walk, so we'll see the city?"

" What do you prefer?" I'm already looking around.

"Alright, come on," she says and moves forward. I go after her, carrying my bag in one hand. I hope to fill this bag with wonderful memories. I get lost in the beauty of Florence. It is truly magical, and I can't believe that this is happening to me. I don't believe that I'm experiencing this. The city is so lively, so cheerful, and so dynamic. Pisa is a quieter place, a much smaller town, but I like Florence. I see so many beautiful things that I forget about everything else. I think the impression of the city overcomes my fears, at least for now.

"Enzo, are you okay?" Leah shouts out in front of me. She's as comfortable as someone who is native to Florence. She's doing great, and I have a feeling that she can fit in anywhere.

"It's great, I like it a lot," I smile. "Leah, how are you doing this?"

"Doing what?" she says but doesn't stop hurrying.

"You're so confident, you're doing so great. You're not from Florence, yet you act as if Florence is yours."

"Enzo, we have no choice but to be brave. I don't want to spend my life in fear, you understand? I go into the unknown, I explore, I make mistakes, I fall, and I get up again. It's like that all the time, but I don't stop. I don't want to observe my own life. I want to live it."

"Yes," I confirm, knowing what she means.

I walk behind her bravely, as if I want to drink in all her energy. It's amazing how Leah seems to possess some magical power that moves me, and soars high into the sky. I feel it every second, and when I'm closest to the bottom and I want to stay there and not move, she knows how to say the right thing that changes my perspective. She knows how to get me to fight for what belongs to me. After meeting Leah however, I realised that my dreams don't have to be limited or colourless, they can be anything. I have the right to desire anything and to believe that it belongs to me. It's part of human nature to have great and wonderful dreams. It's in the nature of man to want to dream and to desire, and it's in the nature of man to dream and strive for things. What is completely unnatural is to deprive ourselves of the things we secretly crave, on the pretext that we don't deserve them. It is a man who is selfish towards himself, and bad to his own soul, even though he desperately wants to be nurtured, who behaves that way. If the soul is the core of man, then it is the balance of happiness that needs to be maintained constantly. The nurturing of the soul consists of listening to the soul, it is the faith that man must have in the soul, and in the communication between man and the soul.

I didn't communicate with my soul for a long time. I was angry at my soul for no reason. I had to get angry at someone, so I got angry at my soul. My soul was patient, and incredibly careful with me, waiting for me to realise that I should not be angry, that I was wrong and that my soul was not the place where I should aim my fury. My soul waited for a long time for me to wake up, but finally got tired too.

One day, my soul stopped waiting for me, stopped understanding me, stopped tolerating me, and stopped listening to me. My soul seemed to disappear overnight, and turned into a black hole which swallowed me in one breath, and I sank hopelessly. That black hole covered me with its darkness and extinguished every little light I carried within me, even the spark from my eyes stopped shining. I was swallowed in that hole for too long. That dark hole is my shell, in which neither the birds sing, nor the music is heard, nor the joy is felt. A glimmer of hope appeared suddenly in the black hole when Leah appeared in my life. In disbelief, I began to cling to that crumb of hope, and that crumb grew a little every day. I know that it's possible for that crumb to grow into something big, something which I can climb onto to finally get out of the black hole. I know it's really possible, but I also know it's incredibly difficult and complex. If that ever happens I may be able to snatch some light from the outside world and throw that light into the black hole. That hole was once my soul, and I want to illuminate it, I want to cheer it up, so that it can forgive me and come back to me. I sigh and let my thoughts weave stories in my head. Leah is still moving incredibly fast, and I can't believe I'm still able to follow her.

"Leah, are we close?" I gasp.

"A little more, a little more," she laughs.

"Okay," I say, and keep going. I try to be fast, and I don't want to think that I don't have the strength to do this, so I keep talking. "Leah, what is the name of our hotel?"

"The hotel is called Balestri," she replies.

"It's in the centre of town, isn't it?"

"Yes, it's centrally located. It's only a ten-minute walk from Piazza della Signoria. The hotel is great, it overlooks the river Arno. Our room has a terrace and a beautiful view."

"I can't wait to see," I smile, not even believing my own excitement.

"A little bit further, let's hurry, Enzo," Leah challenges me, and I suddenly find strength in myself to accelerate. I'm so fast all of a sudden that Leah can't believe it either. I can't believe it, my legs are faster than I thought, and my stamina is more enduring than I could have guessed. I begin to think that man often underestimates his abilities, because man can do much more than he thinks. I don't know if there is a hidden force that lives in us, or maybe there is a reserve power that appears occasionally, but today when I see how fast I am, I am sure that I'm much more than myself. Enzo is really much stronger than he realises, and Enzo is much bigger than Enzo realises. I must never forget that."

"Here we are, we've arrived," Leah rejoices and points.

I see the hotel and new feelings awaken in me. I'm excited, I'm happy, and I'm a little scared, but I'm incredibly present. It seems to me that I can touch and see all the feelings that swim in me. The image I see in front of me is so clear. I can feel the moment. I exist completely.

"It is so beautiful, Leah, really," I tell her.

"I know, I know," she looks at me proudly. "Come on," she says as she enters the hotel, and I follow her.

Leah confidently announces our arrival at reception while I get lost in the beauty of the hotel. I feel like a small, lost child in a world full of toys. I memorise every detail, and I can't stop admiring everything around me. There are many people in the main hall of the hotel, all speaking different languages and in a hurry. There is a large bar next to the comfortable armchairs, and there is a piano beside it. Several couples sit here and drink wine while a man plays music. The atmosphere is romantic and very pleasant. The hotel is full of bright and shiny decorations, and I am completely immersed in the beauty and smell of a new beginning.

"Enzo, do you like it?"

"Yes, it's wonderful," I'm impressed.

"Are we going to our room? I have the key," she smiles at me.

"Is everything all right?" I ask her, suddenly feeling extremely nervous.

"Yes, yes, everything is fine. Are we going?"

I think until this moment, I didn't realise that on this trip Leah and I will be in the same room. I have never slept next to her and I have never slept with her. Our greatest and deepest intimacy comes down to a kiss and a touch, and now I'm starting to get scared.

"Leah, I have to tell you, I'm a little scared now that I realise what's happening. Maybe we are in a hurry, maybe it's not the right time. I don't know what I thought when I agreed to come on this trip, I really don't know!"

I begin to sweat and speak in a slightly higher tone. The guests at the hotel notice my reaction, but I'm too nervous at the moment to worry about anything.

"Enzo, what's happening to you? We came to Florence, everything is wonderful. We have a beautiful room, in a great hotel. Florence is lovely, and I can't wait for us to explore it together. What are you afraid of?" she approaches me, clasping my hands tightly.

"Leah, I cannot ..."

"Enzo, calm down, listen to me, I will never betray you. I wanted us to come here together, because I know it's good for you and I know you're ready. I see it, and you'll see it soon. Please, I just want you to believe me. Can you believe that?" she says with tears in her eyes.

I tremble and I get lost again, the same feeling I had earlier comes over me, like it never left me at all, and suddenly I feel too weak. I think I'll get lost any moment now, but Leah holds my hands tightly and doesn't let go.

"Enzo, nothing bad will happen to you, nothing! The worst is over, my Enzo, now a life full of beauty awaits you! Enzo, don't leave me now, please, don't you see how close we are?" she says as I tremble.

I'm filled with fear and trembling. I see my own face in her beautiful eyes and I'm ashamed of what I see.

"This is not me, this is not who I want to be," I say through tears.

"Then don't' be, it's very simple, it's much

simpler than you think, my Enzo! Don't be someone you don't like, don't be what you don't want to be! Be proud of yourself, be the best, be the biggest, be full of colourful colours and take the grey out of yourself!"

She hugs me tightly.

"Yes!" I tremble and try to stay in the moment. I stay present, no matter how much it hurts, no matter how much something hurts me inside, I stay put. I don't allow myself to lose, I don't accept the Enzo I saw in Leah's eyes. I don't want to be him, I don't want to! I calm down until I can breathe again. The difficult seconds pass, and suddenly I see clearly again.

" Did it pass?" she asks me, knowing I feel better.

"Yes," I say.

"Can we go to our room now? I want you to see the beautiful view," she smiles at me, squeezing my hands again.

"Come on," I tell her boldly, feeling confident, tired of the constant unrest, and we move on. At the moment I don't think of anything. We enter the elevator and go to our room on the third floor. As we enter our room, Leah puts her small suitcase down and jumps on the bed with her arms outstretched.

"Enzo, isn't it wonderful?" she exclaims.

Hypnotised by it all, I head to the terrace. I open the door and step out. The Arno River is spread out before my eyes. The look gives me so much peace and some hope. I take a deep breath and I close my eyes; it's magical. I feel like I'm a white sheet of paper, completely clean and unwritten. My life begins now, and everything that happened up until now is being erased. A gentle breeze seems to caress me, and I smile.

In fact, we are all longing for a new beginning. We all want a new piece of paper to rewrite our story. I long for that too, I'm terribly entangled in the old strings. I want to breathe like this every day, I want to be able to sigh freely and catch my breath again. I love my whole life, with all its parts and all its meanings. I no longer want to be an observer, I want my soul back. I want to calm down with my soul.

"How about this room?" she asks, and hugs me, wrapping her arms around my waist, and kissing my neck. "Do you like it?" She whispers to me and I start to blush. I feel shy, but I don't move.

"It's perfect, perfect," I whisper.

"Tonight we can sit here on the terrace, talk, and drink wine," she kisses me again.

"Maybe."

"And now, let's start the day and see Florence," she says while she gives me soft little kisses.

"Yes, we are only here today anyway, I want to make the most of the time," I say, agreeing with her, and she looks at me in astonishment.

"I want to. I know you don't believe me, but I really do," I smile.

"I know you want to, and I trust you, I will always trust you. I see you and I put my belief in you, because I knew that we would get here. I knew that one day we would start living so much, that one life would seem so small to you," she says, "I'm ready in five minutes. Get organised, so we can go out, can we?"

I open my bag to take out a clean t-shirt, and go to the bathroom to change into it. I look in the mirror and smile.

"I know this Enzo from somewhere," I mutter to myself.

Chapter14

Leah and I walk through the streets of Florence, carefree. I can't believe what beauty I see in front of me. We move through the city centre, which is filled with crowds, locals, rushing to places or relaxing in restaurants. There are tourists too, who don't stop taking photos.

"Enzo, here is the Cathedral of Florence, the Duomo di Florence, look how magical it is," Leah says.

I've heard about this cathedral from my parents, I've researched it myself too, so I know it's one of the biggest attractions in Florence. I stand in front of the Cathedral and completely allow myself to be amazed by its beauty. This is the first time I see it in front of me, but I already have a lot of information about this cathedral. I also know that it's the fourth largest church in the world.

"There are so many people waiting in line to get in, one would think entry is free," Leah says.

"It's free," I add with confidence.

"How do you know?"

"I know," I continue to look at the cathedral without blinking.

"Enzo, I'm going to start thinking you've been to Florence before," she laughs.

I'm silent in response.

I haven't been to Florence, but I wish I had visited here at some point in my life, instead of just staying home. I think that might change a lot of things.

"Do you want to go in?" she asks me.

"No, we're going to waste a lot of time, and if you don't mind, I'm more inclined to enter Piazza della Signoria, Palazzo Vecchio," I say.

She looks at me with surprise.

"You know everything, don't you?"

"Yes, I read about these places. Palazzo Vecchio is a place I've long wanted to visit. I

want to see the museum on the inside. You know
I love art."

"I know, I know," she looks at me like she
admires that, "but why didn't you say anything,
why didn't you mention anything when we talk
about Florence?"

"I didn't want to say anything because I didn't
know if I'd be able to get here, do you
understand?" I look at her.

"I understand," she smiles at me. "I
understand and I'm happy. Come on, do we
continue?"

"Maybe," I smile.

We start from Piazza del Duomo, going all the
way to Piazza della Signoria. Leah is amazed at
all the facts know about Florence and its
landmarks, and I can't wait to get to the Palazzo
Vecchio.

"Enzo, were your parents at the museum?" she
asks me as we walk.

"Yes, they were," I answer.

"Did they like it?" she continues.

"I don't know, my parents and I don't talk
about art."

"How can you not speak to them about that?
Do they know that you paint?"

"Leah, I don't paint, I did paint and when I

was painting, my parents were less interested in that than anything else they could be uninterested in."

"I think you're wrong, your parents love you and they certainly loved your talent," she said challenging my opinion.

"Leah, what kind of talent are you talking about?" I get annoyed. "There is no such thing anymore, it's lost, it's dead. Do you understand? Stop looking for what's not in me, stop!" I turn my head to the other side, unable to calm down.

She stands behind me, hugs me at my waist, and then closes her eyes. I don't understand what's happening, but I'm so nervous that I don't want to ask her anything.

"Keep going; when we stop, I'll open your eyes and you'll see what's in front of you. If your heart doesn't beat like never before, then come and tell me that what I'm looking for in you is dead, and I'll believe you," she whispers to me as we walk.

I'm still nervous, but I agree and don't object. First we walk for a bit, and then suddenly she opens my eyes. I look around, and I'm standing on Piazza della Signoria. In front of me I see the Palazzo Vecchio.

My nervousness dissipates, and my whole

body is at peace and tranquil. I see the beautiful building and am overcome with such strong emotions that I can hardly help but cry with happiness. The euphoria, the joy, the warmth, and the truth seem to merge into one small ball, which tirelessly rolls through my body, making me shudder with excitement. Leah puts her hand on my heart. "It's tireless. It rejoices. It lives," she says, and I look at her and smile, knowing that she's telling me the truth.

"Look how beautiful it is, Enzo, just look!"

She spins in a circle in front of me. I think it's wonderful too, it's really wonderful. I wanted to come here for such a long time, but I never told anyone, even today, when Leah and I were travelling to Florence, I didn't want to say anything because I was scared. I just wanted to get to Florence. Now I stand on the square of Piazza della Signoriaand see all the beauty with my own eyes.

There's no need for anyone to tell me how it is in Florence, there's no need for my parents to come home with countless memories and share them with me, while I feel trapped in my own body, at the same time feeling incredibly guilty that I'm not trying to change the situation. If my parents could see me in this moment, I don't know if they would be proud of me or maybe they'd remain indifferent. They might ask themselves a few questions and hesitate about the answers. I would certainly smile at them.

"Enzo, are we going?" Leah asks.

"Yes," I reply, and we walk along the square, heading to the entrance of the palace. On the right I see the well-known, open gallery of sculptures Loggia dei Lanzi, with the three large arches, which look like a miracle to me.

"What was the name of this? I knew, but I forgot," Leah sounds a bit confused.

"Loggia dei Lanzi, an open gallery of sculptures," I explain, and she looks at me in amazement again.

"Enzo, you really know everything," she laughs at me, and I kiss her on the cheek. We approach the entrance of the palace, the place where the tickets are sold. There are a lot of people, but the queue is moving fast. We stand in line and I can't wait to get in. I'm impatient. Leah looks around, carefree, enjoying every moment happening to her. When I see her doing that, I really envy her. I have a feeling that she doesn't expect anything at all, but she gets everything. It's more evidence that I'm looking for the things I lack, in vain, because that way

I'll never find them. I slowly stop with my vain expectations, thoughts, requests, disappointments, and try to feel every moment of life. I think I'm on the right track, and I know Leah thinks the same.

"Welcome," the woman who sells tickets addresses me.

"Two tickets to the museum and the tower," I say, and Leah looks at me, shocked, not even blinking.

The woman hands me the tickets and I leave the queue holding it in my hands. I still can't believe what's happening to me. I'm very happy and excited, and completely surprised by myself.

"Enzo, you bought the tickets so confidently, you looked very independent and safe, you know?" she hugs me, sneaking a peek at the tickets.

"Yes," I look at her and feel proud.

"Yes!" she exclaims excitedly. "Let's start," she says and walks in front of me.

I sink into the world of art as we enter the museum. I feel completely calm and safe being surrounded by something so familiar to my spirit. The very smell of the museum evokes memories in me. I stop for a moment and take a deep breath, the same way I took a breath on the hotel terrace, looking at the Arno River. My lungs are filled with art and creative energy, and I, like a magician, walk through the space, unable to stop rejoicing in the beauty around me.

"How magical, Enzo!" Leah says thoughtfully. "What do you know about this palace? You probably know some interesting facts," she says.

"The Medici family lived here and decorated it completely, turning the space into a mysterious palace. It takes you into many courtyards, hidden corridors, terraces, and rooms, like a labyrinth. You will see the walls are decorated with works by unique artists and painters like Michelangelo and Donatello." I talk as we move forward. Leah follows me and turns around in a circle in the huge hall, paying attention to all the details around her. We separate from each other for a moment, and I start moving around alone. Quite unintentionally, as if hypnotised, I get lost in all the beauty. I climb to the first floor and my adventure continues, staring at the unique works on the walls, as if I'm floating through time and standing in the centre of the Renaissance. I walk through the rooms, and I walk through the corridors. I really feel like I'm in a maze. It's wonderful, and every corner has its own story.

The feeling is indescribable. My heart beats faster than usual, my hands are shaking, but this time, out of happiness and excitement, and I can't take the smile off my face. I keep going forward, exploring and drinking from the art displays and the creativity. I can't stop admiring everything I see.

"How happy I am to be here!" I murmur as I walk through the museum looking at the beautiful rooms, each one different from the next, each decorated in a special way. Architecture and art seem to merge into one in this palace, and each creates its own wonder.

My legs glide unconsciously, and I can't stop feeling excitement. I'm impatient, and I want to see everything. I don't know where Leah is, but I'm sure we'll find each other soon again. I don't know why, but for the first time I feel I want to be alone a little, and I want to experience what I see by myself.

I keep looking around, while I hear all the people inside the palace make sounds of admiration. Everyone is obviously carried away by the beauty they see. The palace is huge, so there is no big crowd in one particular place. I have a feeling that people are somehow evenly distributed throughout. Going up to the second floor, I fall more and more in love with art and architecture. I know I'm moving a little fast, but I can't beat my impatience.

I'm in such disbelief that I think everything will disappear in a second, so I want to grab this whole experience as soon as possible. I don't want it to end. I never want this to end! I move forward, moving through the palace, and every moment brings me a million wonderful new moments that I'll never forget. I jump, and I can't even explain why. After a long time, I feel something for the first time, as if a completely new story is pouring into me and I have the right to experience it as I wish. It's a feeling of incredible freedom, and I lost my freedom and was without it for a long time. Now I fly. I feel like I fly all the time, and I'm completely free.

"I want to climb the tower!" I mutter to myself.

I'm trying to find the stairs to the tower, but I can't find it. I ask one of the palace staff, and he shows me where to go. I follow his instructions, and manage easily. I'm just too impatient that's all, so I walk too fast. I find the stairs leading to the top of the tower and start climbing. I'm in such a hurry, as if I have no air, and the air I need is at the top of the tower. I climb, and I can hardly breathe, but I don't stop. There are a lot of stairs, but it doesn't scare me at all, because I climbed the previous ones without feeling any difficulty.

I climb, and I climb, until I can almost smell the air. I can almost peek at the beautiful view from above with one eye. I'm in a hurry, and I'm almost there. I climb the last stairs. I arrive, and I can hardly breathe, but it doesn't matter to me at all. I stop at the stone windows, and I try to find a place. There are many people who admire the view. I push between them and for a moment, I manage to see the beautiful view over all of Florence, with my own eyes.

The whole city is in front of me, and the cathedral looks so close, it's almost as if I can touch it. Florence is closer to me than ever before. I feel that I can lie on the whole city, and the happiness I feel inside me will cover me and make me sleep. I turn left, I turn right, I want to take this beautiful view with me forever. At the moment, I start thinking about something else, and some new thoughts cross my mind.

"Why did my parents never bring me here?" I mutter. "Why did they never take me with them to visit Florence the countless times they came? Why? Why did they never bring me to this palace, when they knew how much I love art?

Why did they just tell me about their wonderful journeys and never let me be a part of it? Why did they leave me to read about this place when they could simply bring me? Why did they torture me like that? Why?! Why did they leave me with that horrible woman? Why did they leave me with her every time? My mind travels to that terrible thought, that frightening woman, who preferred to touch my underwear rather than look after me like she was paid to do?! Why?" I scream it out loud in front of all of Florence. Everyone around me notices, but no one dares to approach me. I cry, and I can't stop my tears. I fall on my knees, huddled in the corner.

People around me are scared and ask me if I need help, but I refuse. One of the employees approaches me and offers me help, but I ask him to leave me because that is the only way I will calm down. I can hardly hear them talking to me, I start to get lost again. My body stays in place, but I feel like I'm disappearing and floating through space again. I get lost, I get completely lost. I can think of nothing but how much I need Leah right now.

"Leah, Leah!" I murmur, and think my tears will slowly drown me. "Leah, Leah," I continue. I close my eyes and I'm already quite close to the moment when I know my happiness will disappear. I'm approaching the beginning of the tunnel and I know there is no light inside.

"Enzo, Enzo, what's the matter with you, Enzo?!" suddenly Leah hugs me and squeezes me hard. "It's okay, calm down. Please calm down. Nothing is terrible, nothing happened, the worst is over. Calm down," she tells me, and I close my eyes again. "Enzo, please just listen to me. We're not in a hurry. We'll be here until you feel better. Please just don't stop listening to me, okay?!" she kisses me, trying to open my eyes.

I slowly open the lids and vaguely see Leah kneeling in front of me, completely scared and pale. She doesn't stop talking to me, and I try not to stop listening to her.

"Enzo, this had to happen, now it will be easier, believe me," she smiles. "You're overcoming your fear Enzo, you're fighting with yourself. Enzo, you will win."

"You mean it?" I ask anxiously.

"I'm sure," she replies.

"Leah, I was walking alone through the palace, I left you, forgive me. I'm a fool for thinking I can walk alone, look what happened," I apologise.

"Enzo, I left you on purpose because I saw

how much you enjoyed it and I know it was important for you to experience all this alone. Enzo, you're strong enough, you don't need me, you're completely capable of everything, believe me!" she says.

"But, Leah, I broke down ..."

"Yes, and got up again, you are here again, you come back again. You know what? I'm happy you broke down, and I hope that you broke down the scared Enzo, who doesn't look like you at all!"

"Yes," I bow my head and already feel a little better. I crashed into the tallest tower in Florence," I smile.

"You hit the ground well. My Enzo, after such an end, there's nothing to follow but a new beginning," she kisses me.

.   .   .

The day in Florence is slowly coming to an end. Time passes faster and faster after visiting the Palazzo Vecchio. We walk through the centre of town, grab some delicious pizza, and walk some more. I hold Leah by the hand as we explore the beautiful city, but I see that she no longer has the strength.

"Are you tired?" I ask her.

"A little," she smiles at me.

"It was a wonderful day. I'm so happy I came here with you Leah, no matter what happened, nothing would change that. I saw Florence, I felt the magic of this city, I saw wonderful things, and I experienced unique moments. "I'm grateful."

"Enzo, I'm so happy for you and for the life that still awaits you," she squeezes my hands tightly.

I'm quiet, and I just hug her. Countless people pass by us, yet I feel like we're alone in the world.

"Enzo, I suggest we go back to the hotel, sit on our magical terrace, enjoy the view while having a nice glass of wine, and some delicious food. What do you think?" she looks at me.

"Sure," I agree without thinking. I really want to sit down for a while, because it was a long day for me.

We leave for the hotel, and I don't stop holding her hand. I breathe the air of Florence and I feel great. I'm thinking about the day I had, and I can't believe I'm still here. Now I'm sure I'm stronger than before. I really feel different. There was a time when every time I crashed, I couldn't go back. It still hurts, and will probably hurt forever, but my desire for life is greater than any pain that can inflict me. I live. I live like this, as I lived today. I live a real life every day. I love daily, full of vicissitude and complication, full of unpredictable moments, full of temptation and beauty. I know now that while I was looking at all those people from my window, despising their lives, it was in fact only the anger in me speaking.

All I wanted was to be able to do the same things, to walk the streets, to talk to people, to have things happen to me, to have something to tell, instead of just being told. Today I'm one of those people, today I do things too, today new things happen to me, today I am an interesting person who can tell an interesting story to someone.

"We're close, Enzo, we're close," Leah tells me as we walk the streets around the centre of town of beautiful Florence.

"Great," I smile at her, and she kisses me.

"Enzo, I want to ask you something," she continues.

"Here you are."

"What do you think would've happened if I hadn't come upstairs to the tower when I did?"

"What do I think?" I'm confused.

"You were alone in the Palazzo Vecchio, and you were walking. You were fine, and then I was suddenly gone. You climbed to the top of the tower, and saw the view. You looked at Florence, and it was beautiful. What if the same thing happens to you today? Let's say I'm gone, and you're alone again. What do you think would happen?" Leah says confusing me even more.

"I would die, for sure. I would die in the worst way, without dying physically. I would die within myself, leaving only my body alive," I say bowing my head. Leah stands in front of me and puts her two gentle hands on my head, lifting my face to hers to look her straight in the eyes.

"Enzo, you would not die. It would bring you to life. It would certainly bring you to life, just as it did today."

"Leah, this is my first time going there, I've never dared go before. If you weren't here to hug me and comfort me, I couldn't do it alone ..."

"Enzo, I didn't tell you anything new. You know it all. You carry it all in your soul. You went there for the first time and it had to happen. You yourself know that you had to touch that point within yourself. You had to feel that pain again, to let it go. Enzo, don't you see that I have nothing to do with it?! This is you, this is just you," she hugs me and starts crying.

My tears start to flow, and we both tremble beside each other, fused into one, as if we are one soul. I can swear that in my chest I feel something strange. It is as if a wave in me became calm, and woke up. It is as if a blow from inside hit me, and I wasn't scared at all. I've been accustomed to a calm sea and a monotonous flat line in which nothing happens for a long time, and the restless wave in me is like spring after a long and cold winter.

I don't know how, but I just know that nothing will be the same again. I know that my peaceful sea is a finished story, and I know I'll get a whole new story. This wave that I feel is the beginning of a series of other tireless waves, which will completely move me in new directions. I feel the cold winter and the grey colouring my world will slowly disappear from me, and spring will bring me a countless blossoming of flowers that will brighten my life beautifully. The scent of joy will intoxicate me, and awaken my soul. It will be a new awakening.

We enter the hotel and people gather in the hall, enjoying quiet piano music and a glass of wine. We go up to our room, and Leah immediately tries to organise everything.

"We'll drink, Prosecco, okay? Do you know what that is?" she laughs as she sits on the bed in our room, holding the phone in her hand.

"I know what it is. It's my parents' favourite. Yes," I answer immediately, coming out onto the terrace, enchanted by the view of the river Arno.

Leah is silent, and although I turn my back on her, I can feel that she's looking at me confused. She is still silent, and I'm still overshadowed by the beauty in front of me.

"Leah, I want to be like water," I say changing the subject, and entering the room.

"Why?" she asks, while she is still holding the phone in her hand.

"Because water is colourless, and that's beautiful," I continue.

"Do you want to be colourless?" she wonders.

"Well, yes. When I think about it, yes I want to be colourless," I say confidently.

"What will happen to all the colours then?" she asks.

"What colours?"

"What will happen to all the colours inside you? What will happen to all the colours you carry within you that make you who you are? Will you forget them, will you delete them?"

"My colours are what I love the most when I

have them, and what I miss the most when I don't have them. Do you know what it's like to live with all those colours and for them to suddenly disappear? It's awful. Colourlessness is something else. When you are colourless, you're simply colourless, that is your constant, and you have nothing to fear," I bow my head.

"But then you have nothing to live for either," she scolds me.

"Leah," I sigh. "I just want to say that it certainly hurts less when you are colourless," I sit on the bed.

"Enzo, I know this day and this place are very important to you," she says as she approaches me, placing her hand on mine.

"You know?" I begin to tremble.

"Yes, that is why I understand what you're saying, but I want you to know something else. One day, you'll realise that your colours are what pushed you through the darkness and what didn't allow you to give up. Colours are the most beautiful thing that can happen to a person, please never doubt it," she gets even closer to me, and I don't stop trembling.

"At times I hate my colours. I think they're to blame for everything. I curse them, and I want to destroy them, then after that, I realise that without them, I don't exist. I realise without them I don't know who I am, so I'm constantly turning around and around in a circle, non-stop."

"Your colours are not to blame for anything, and neither are you. This is your life and your path. You know Enzo, it's simple. We all aim for the same goal. We all want to be happy. One person is closer to this goal, another person is further from this goal, one person reaches their goal fast, and someone else, slower. The point is we're all doing the same thing, basically. We're all looking for our happiness."

Leah is so close to me that it seems like we're completely melting into each other. It's so nice when I hear her talk to me, and I get so shy when she gets so close to me. I want her to be next to me, but I'm afraid of what might happen. After all, I'm not afraid of anything as much as I'm afraid of myself and my own fears. I'm afraid my frustration will eat me up and ruin everything. I want to defeat all of my demons, but I'm afraid they're buried so deep inside me that digging them will bury me in my own hole.

"Enzo, the night is young," Leah says noticing my nervousness. She goes over to the phone and picks it up again. "So, I'm ordering Prosecco, and something to eat. Can I choose different cheeses?" she asks me and laughs sweetly.

"Yes," I say, and sigh a little. Suddenly, it's easier for me.

"Leah, I'm going to the bathroom to change and take a shower, while you order."

I take a clean t-shirt and shorts from my bag, go to the toilet, and close the door. The toilet is compact, but very nice and tidy. There are colourful tiles with irregular dark lines on them, a nice light, a small bathtub, and a mirror with a sink that has a unique oblong shape. The whole hotel is decorated tastefully. I stand in front of the mirror and look at myself. My face is somehow refreshed, and my eyes are wide open. I can see the liveliness of my eyes and cheeks, and I definitely notice some inexplicable change.

The feeling of looking in the mirror and not being able to see yourself at all is horrible and scary. I've experienced this feeling countless times, but now when I look at myself, and can't seem to recognise who I see in the mirror, I feel happy.

I think about how I feel about people who live their lives. These people do different things every day, and every time they want to look in the mirror, they see themselves. It's a real blessing, it's an irreplaceable joy.

I let the tap run. I just want to hear the sound of water, and then I close it again. I take my clothes off and get into the shower. I turn on the shower, and the water is too hot for a moment, but I regulate it. I look at the hotel bath products in the left corner on the shelf and pick one of it. I read that it's a shower gel and I open it.

I pour it all over my body. It smells like fruit, some sweet fruit. It smells good, and I decide I like it. I spread the gel all over my skin and foam it up. It's wonderful, and I enjoy it like a small child. I stand in the shower and the water slowly cleans all the foam off me. My skin seems to glow.

The smell of fruit is incredibly strong, and the whole toilet smells beautiful. I begin to think about the simplicity of what is happening to me and the happiness it brings me. Leah is right. We all seek our happiness. Happiness is found in even the simplest things, such as showering with a gel with the scent of sweet fruit. I can feel that happiness very strongly in this moment. Maybe I wish my mind and my pain can be cleansed as easily as the foam cleanses my body. Maybe I wish I had something to cleanse me from the inside, just like this shower cleanses me from the outside.

Maybe I just want some other things, some other dimensions to my life, and some other rules. It doesn't matter. My happiness is in the moment and the simplicity is undeniable. All the little things are associated with something else, and that is why at its core, little things bring forth the greatest happiness, I guess.

I get out of the shower and wipe myself off with a towel. The towel is soft and comfortable on my skin. The hotel pays attention to everything, that much is obvious. I look in the mirror again, without intending to, completely by accident, and I manage to see myself this time. I smile.

"Look how clean I am, and look how nice I smell," I murmur contentedly.

Next to the sink there are several products, among them, a small container of body milk. It's interestingly packaged in a little green bottle. I open it and smell the scent. It smells like the shower gel I just used, like some sweet fruit.

"A whole collection, of course," I murmur, admiring the hotel's attention to detail. I pour the body milk into my hand and slowly rub it over my body. The smell is irresistible, and my skin has never been softer. I feel wonderful. I finish rubbing it into my skin and start to get dressed.

The clothes stick to my skin. My skin feels tender today. I look in the mirror again, and I look at the skin on my face, noticing how much it shines today, somehow. My beard is a little longer, but I still look pretty average, unlike the way I used to. I touch my face with my hands. I can feel my skin completely, and feel so connected to myself. My hair is also beautiful. I dry it a little with the towel and let it dry further on its own. I feel present, completely present.

It's time to get out of the bathroom. Leah must have already organised everything on the terrace. I sigh loudly, filling my lungs with air as much as I can.

"I'm brave, I'm aware, I'm alive," I whisper and leave the bathroom.

"Enzo, how beautiful you are. Was the shower okay?" she greets me with a smiling face.

"Yes," I say, a little embarrassed.

"Was it nice?" she asks me.

"What do you think?"

"Well, were you comfortable?"

"Yes, yes. The bathroom is really beautiful. I took a shower, and they have these lovely little sweet-smelling gels and lotions," I smile.

"I know, I can smell the scent on you. You smell wonderful. I'll take a shower later, I just want to relax and enjoy myself now. Come on, come out onto the terrace," she says.

I follow her out onto the terrace, and I am immediately speechless. There are candles on the table, a large plate full of different cheeses, a bottle of, Prosecco, and two glasses. The picture I see in front of me is like a scene from a romantic movie. The view of the river Arno makes the picture even more beautiful. I feel really excited, and instantly less nervous.

"Leah, this looks perfect!" I exclaim, and immediately hug her.

"This is a special night, Enzo," she looks at me and kisses me.

"Is it special?" I'm confused again.

Leah can sometimes say things, leaving me unsure of what she means.

"Yes," she says, and sits on my chair.

I get nervous and I sit down too, but I try to relax, and I try to enjoy what is happening around me and to me. I'm happy. I'm happy all the time, but I'm scared of that happiness as well. I have a feeling that some things are changing, I have a feeling that some things are changing right now, and I'll see that later. Suddenly, nothing will be the same. That much I'm sure of.

"Have you tried Prosecco?" she asks, as she

decants it from the bottle into two glasses.

"I haven't, but the taste was described to me in detail, so I feel like I've tried it," I smile shyly.

"Your parents, right? You told me it was their favourite," she says, raising her glass, bringing it closer to mine, then she says, "toast!"

"Yes, it is their favourite. They told me about the wonderful evenings they spent in Florence, drinking a good Prosecco, constantly. They said they laughed so much that their stomachs ached, and that with good company and a good Prosecco, everything was much easier. Well, I suppose they're right. Here you and I are, we are good company to each other, we drink a good Prosecco, and everything is really much easier."

I lower my head, and suddenly I seem to lose my voice. I stop talking. I wish the conversation on this topic would end, and we could start talking about something else, but I know that won't happen.

"Why are you speaking in the past tense?" she looks at me. "Your parents don't tell you stories anymore?"

"They tell me for sure, there are many new stories that happened to them lately. Only I don't listen anymore. In the beginning, my attitude was intentional, but now I have no control over it. I used to switch off, thinking it would hurt less, and now I am turned off permanently, not able to go back at all," I take a sip from the glass and close my eyes.

"Enzo, you left so you can come back and be even stronger," she says approaching my chair and sits beside me, kneeling before me. She puts her head on my lap. I start stroking her soft, long hair. I hear her breathing deeply in step with my breathing, as if we agreed to take our breaths at the same time.

"Leah, do you think I'll ever get back to being that way? Honestly. Tell me. Do you think I can put my whole life together again?" I ask.

She raises her head from my knees and looks me straight in the eye.

"Enzo, you have to realise that we all fall apart at certain times in our lives, for different reasons," she says. "Things change. We learn from everything that happens to us. You know what? You can always start over. This is your hope. This is your light to focus on. The balance in the world exists, and the brave always get a second chance. The pain of disintegration is horrible, but only he who has felt it has the privilege of feeling the freshness of a new beginning."

I kiss her. I kiss her as hard as I can. I hug her, and I don't want to let her go. I never want to let her go.

"Is Florence really as beautiful as you were told?" she says changing the subject and laughing. She returns to her chair, picks at some pieces of cheese, and waits for me to answer.

"It is beautiful, I have no words actually," I say, and also pick up some cheese.

"But now you understand that things look very different when they happen to others, right?" she continues.

"What do you mean?" I ask. Leah is confusing me.

"As you watched people through your window, believing all things in the world were the same, anger spoke to you, but now that you've visited Florence yourself, do you see you may be wrong about that at the end of the day? The difference we desperately seek is hidden within ourselves. Sooner or later, everyone comes to that conclusion, but it's very important to live in the meantime, not to be angry and closed. It's particularly important to listen, to see each other, to learn from each other, to be informed, and to find out, instead of running away from the unknown and thinking that everything is clear to us. That's how you stay in the same place, that's how you don't soar to great heights."

I listen with my head low, and remain silent.

"We humans tend to overestimate the things that happen to others, thinking that wonderful things happen to everyone except us. It's not true, it's just a distorted perception that bites your soul and bothers you even more, not allowing you to fight. The distorted perception stems from ignorance."

"Leah, nothing was happening to me, while life was happening to everyone around me. I don't overestimate that, it just is, and it hurts, it hurts incredibly much. It leaves traces of teeth, which changed the whole surface of my soul. The bite made my soul uneven, disintegrated it, left me in pieces. I didn't defend it. I didn't protect my soul, not even once."

"I'm talking to you about something else, and you persistently fail to look the truth in the eye. I'm talking to you about your focus and what you should focus on. Tell me, why did you do that to yourself? Why did you put salt in your own wound? Why did you keep thinking about things that you knew would get you nowhere? Why do we damn humans think we need to compare ourselves to each other? What is the misconception that makes us believe that someone else is better? Why do we think we have time in this one life to spend admiring other people's lives and crying over our own?! Isn't that suicide? Isn't it a lynching of one's own spirit and mind? You know what Enzo, Florence is beautiful, but there are many beautiful places in the world, and after a while, all the beauty just repeats itself. After a while, there is no place you can turn into your own refuge, except your own soul and your own thoughts, like your painting, for example. Do you think your painting is less beautiful or less important than a visit to Florence? Do you think that there is a good refuge for you in the world that is better than getting lost in your paintings? Stop underestimating yourself and overestimating the rest of us. Everyone is lost Enzo, absolutely everyone. Unlike you, not everyone has the size of a soul to admit it," she sighs, drinking Prosecco from her glass.

She takes her last sip, then picks up the bottle and refills it, then fills my glass too. I just look at her and say nothing. I want to absorb this moment completely and I want to remember her every word. I think her words are like needles that pass through my skin. It releases some new energy that begins to float through my body and lift me up. I have the strength to fly for a moment. I have the strength to soar high and look at the world from above, to realise that all beauty, after a while, indeed everything repeats itself, and my only refuge may be my soul and my thoughts.

"Cheers! Let's talk about something else," Leah says, and looks out at the Arno River.

"You told me you want to be colourless like this water. Do you still want that?" she looks at me.

"No. I think I'm changing my mind," I reply as I look out to the river.

"You have the right to change your mind, changing your mind is a reflection of growing and maturing. You can't do without your colours, no matter how much they irritate you at times, no matter how much you feel that they sometimes take you down, your colours are your essence and you should be proud of them," she says.

"I know, I understand. Every time, I fall in love with my colours again, but there are times when I wish I didn't have them at all. I don't know why, but I think it's much easier for colourless people."

"You're doing the same thing again, you're idealising what you don't have, forgetting the value of what you do have. We're not all the same, and if you're lucky enough to have colours in you, then you're special. Life shouldn't be easy, it should be interesting, full of challenges and situations that we learn from. Life is like a test, so hopefully you can pass it easily, but it's more than that. Life is a series of exams, tests, puzzles, and crossroads. Your job is to live those moments, to make mistakes, to learn, to repeat, to try, and finally, to win."

"I don't think life is a test. I say that because if it were, I'd pass it no matter how difficult it is. Life is something else. It's like an ordinary day. You think it'll be the same as it was the previous day and the same as every other day, but then, on that one day, everything changes. Nobody asks you about it, nobody warns you about anything.

You're alone, left to the wolf in the forest. The wolf has been hungry for a long time. The wolf has been stalking you, planning the day when he'll get you alone and unprepared, incapable of self-defence, waiting for you to be vulnerable. That one day, is my whole life."

She looks at me with fear in her eyes that she

can't hide. She seems frightened and upset, like she knows everything. I know she knows. I'm sure of it.

"Enzo, did you tell anyone about that wolf? Who is that wolf, Enzo? You have to start talking slowly, this is the only way we'll expel that bad energy from you. This is the only way we will dig out what you buried a long time ago. Don't hide anymore, aren't you tired of it? Discover yourself, express yourself, and relieve yourself of the hurt, my Enzo! When you tell the truth, you will get rid of it forever," she says, as she comes to me, kneels beside me and holds my hands, looking at me, with eyes full of tears.

She squeezes my palms, not allowing me to disappear, not allowing me to evaporate like colourless steam.

"I am not steam! I am full of colours. I am full of the most vivid colours!" I tremble, and she squeezes my hands and encourages me to continue.

"Leah, I can't go back there again, I can't! Leah, if I say anything, I'll disappear. I'm afraid to think about it, let alone say anything. Leah, if I go back there for a second, I'll disappear forever. I can't."

"It won't happen, my Enzo. The worst has

already happened. It couldn't be worse now. You have to face it, you have to win and talk about it. You have to unwind the ball full of evil thoughts and bad energy. Kick that ball full of fear and insecurity, let it fly away from you and never come back! Speak Enzo, please speak. You won't disappear, I promise you won't disappear. I'm here, I'm holding you. I'll never let you go. I'm part of you. I'm you, and you're me," she says as her hands hold me tight and don't allow me to fall.

"Leah, how can I talk about something I want to forget forever? How can I dig up that skeleton after so many years? I can hardly speak without crying."

"If you want to forget something, you have to talk about it first! You have to let all the pain come out of you so you can let go of yourself! Enzo, you underestimate yourself a lot. You can do this, believe me, I know you can do it!" she cries out, unable to calm herself down.

She is tense but still bold and strong, as she kneels before me and refuses to give up, so that I will not give up either.

I take a deep breath and try to control my body. I try to calm down. I breathe, I just try to breathe. I fill my lungs with air, wanting to push the fear out of me. I find all the strength I have in me, and all the strength that Leah gives me. I fight with myself, for myself, as if I'm pushing myself with my own fist. Every part of my body hurts, but I don't want to give up. I want to stay in the moment and see what happens with my own eyes. I'm tired of telling stories.

A wave is rippling through me again and it gives me a signal that Enzo is alive. I detach myself from my own body and look at myself from the side. The sight is sad, I see a man who has just reached the age of thirty, and continues to miss his most beautiful moments, because he is afraid to live. I see a young man who has skilful hands and likes to paint a lot, but instead of playing with his colours, he covers his face with his hands, fearing his grey spirit. I see a young man who regularly slaps his own irreplaceable virtues, thinking that his uniqueness is his greatest shame.

I want to change this sad sight, because it's been around for too long, and I never want to see it again. I return to the zone of my body and touch all the contours of myself. I am completely comfortable with every part of me, it all belongs to me.

"Leah, Mrs. Sofia, Mrs. Sofia is to blame for

everything," I murmur and calm down a bit.

"Who is Mrs. Sofia? Is she the wolf? Is she your wolf? Leah holds me tightly in her palms, not daring to let me go. My hands are sweaty and slippery, and Leah grabs them and wipes them on her dress.

"Yes," I keep muttering.

"That's why you reacted like that to my Sofia," she says, putting the pieces together. "What did that lady Sofia do to you? Tell me. Slow down, don't rush," she encourages me.

"I can't Leah, I'm afraid to remember," I get upset and cry again. I experience an incredible cycle of emotions, like a fast car driving through my feelings and everything is constantly changing.

"Try, come on, start slowly," she continues to encourage me.

I try to calm down and start talking. I swallow my own tears several times, until I finally get together enough courage to speak more.

"One day, one Saturday, my parents were in Florence for a weekend, with friends. I was seven years old. They left me at home with Mrs. Sofia, to take care of me. She worked for my father's company, but after her husband left, she couldn't do the same work anymore. My father didn't want to leave her on the street because she was close to them. My former nanny moved out of Pisa, so Mrs. Sophia took her place. The first few months she worked for us, everything seemed to be fine, but I always felt there was something strange about her. I was very small, but even then I picked up on her negative energy. I tried to tell my parents how I felt about her and asked them to find me another woman to take care of me, not considering the option that I could have asked my parents to spend more time with me themselves.

My parents didn't want to listen to me, they told me to stop talking nonsense and to be nice to Mrs. Sofia. I spent little time with my parents. Even though we were a family, we didn't really know each other. So that day, that Saturday, my parents went to Florence with friends, and I stayed home with Mrs. Sophia, who in the evening, while watching me fall asleep and supposedly protecting me, put her hand in my pyjamas. I didn't know what was happening. I watched her as the prey would look at its wolf. I was confused and scared. I couldn't defend myself. I didn't even know if anyone was attacking me. I watched Mrs. Sofia, who, while moving her hand in my pyjamas, had a smile on her face and closed her eyes from time to time. She made some noises, whispering to me, "Enzo, you are such a nice boy, Enzo, you will be a real man."

I stop talking suddenly, and I need a moment to breathe. I don't cry, and I don't tremble. I just sit on my chair with my head down and wait for something to happen.

"Enzo, did this happen once?" Leah touches my face with one hand and caresses me.

"I don't want you to feel sorry for me, Leah," I look at her, removing her hand from my face.

"I don't feel sorry for you, Enzo. This isn't sad, this is scary. You survived this, that's why I admire you!"

"No, it didn't happen just once. It happened until I was ten, until my mother accidentally resented Mrs. Sophia for something completely different and persuaded my father to fire her. Since then no one has seen or mentioned her."

"You tried to tell your parents what was going on?"

"It took me a while to figure out what was going on. Once I realised; yes, I tried. I tried in my own way, but looking from back from this distance, I'm aware that it wasn't a real attempt. They didn't want to listen to me. I don't blame them. I didn't try to explain to them properly. I wasn't persistent enough, I wasn't brave enough. After facing rejection from them, I decided to bury it within myself. I knew what was done to me was wrong, but I decided to keep quiet. Do you see?! Ever since I was a child, I've had the habit of stacking things in my soul, so that one day it would explode!" I cry again.

"Enzo, you were small, you didn't know."

"No, Leah. I knew! Maybe at first I didn't know, from the beginning I didn't, but after a while I knew I was being abused, and I knew that if I kept silent it would destroy me! I knew that what was happening was evil and I knew that I had the right to persistently try to speak about it and tell the truth, but I didn't. I covered up all the evil that was inflicted on me. I covered all the injustice. I covered all the pain, and do you know where the paradox is, Leah? Although I knew it would destroy me, I secretly hoped it would pass. I hoped that such a thing could pass with time, and that I could forget and live a normal life. I had a damn stupid hope inside myself for something I didn't deserve at all. It never passed. There were only stages. First there was the isolation phase; then the silence phase; then a phase of incredible closeness, and difficult confrontation with reality and its needs; and finally there was the phase of the disease.

This happens to the best of people, the doctor said, trying to encourage me. With a lot of work, he said we will get results and he said I would find my balance. He was right, he was really right. Only on the other side there was a patient who didn't want to co-operate. I was incredibly lost, and at the same time infinitely angry. An angry man doesn't want to help himself, I know that now."

"What about your parents? What happened to them next?"

"I don't know, at one point I was completely lost. I can still hear my mother's worried voice asking the doctor if I will be okay. I can hear her telling the doctor they had to bring me to see him because it was no longer safe for me to be at home. I can hear her asking the doctor how they know I won't do something to myself. I can still hear my father's voice telling the doctor, that before, when there are bad days, it really looks bad, that it is as if I am completely out of control."

"Enzo."

I look at the Arno River and for a moment my body calms down. I don't know if the simplicity of the river calms me or if it is the quiet wind that suddenly starts waving on our terrace. All I know is it brings me something unexpected, and suddenly I can let out my last breath of old pain. I know this is not the last goodbye to pain, because it's now clear to me that I can endure a lot of hurt, and that's probably why it will always be a part of me. Leaving the old pain to make room for the new pain is a step in the right direction though.

The sound of the freshly poured, Prosecco in my glass brings my thoughts back to our terrace, while Leah looks at me and says nothing. As I spoke, I didn't look her in her eyes once, I just couldn't. I drink from my glass, and I stare into it, bolder than ever. We both look at each other and are silent. There is silence, which speaks louder than any words in the world. We both know that we've reached a point which we only hoped to experience. It's a beautiful moment.

"I want to tell you something," Leah tells me, and puts her feet on my lap. She smiles at me and I start stroking her feet. How tender they are, like a new-born's. I'm surprised by her every time. Her beauty is completely spontaneous, and she is perfectly beautiful without any effort. She looks like she is constantly trying to look like this. I can't stop wondering how easily she lives her life, and at the same time she knows exactly what she's doing. She's not lost at all.

"How beautiful your feet are," I tell her, and she keeps laughing.

"I want to tell you something," she says.

"Well, tell me," I say, looking at her in the eyes. I want to see everything, I want to feel everything. I don't want to miss anything. I don't know how to describe the feeling that I suddenly feel so strongly at the moment, but it's an incredible curiosity about everything around me, and a constant interest in my whole environment. Every word, every look, every smile, every touch, every smell, every thought, every move, and every hidden moment, I want to feel it and I never miss anything more.

"I think there comes a time when you will learn to be incredibly happy," she says. I pull her chair closer to mine, approach her, and continue to meet my eyes evenly with hers. She lowers her legs and crosses them on top of each other, as if she is ashamed.

"Leah, I managed to tell someone," I say, stroking her beautiful face as my hands begin to tremble with excitement. "I can't believe it".

"Enzo, you did this on your own. You will see

how important that is. You'll see how it's necessary to face everything you carry inside endlessly, to clean up, and start again," she smiles at me, kissing my hand as I caress her.

"You're right, but if it weren't for you, none of this would have happened. You're the core of my existence and the cause of everything. Every good thing that happened to me, I owe to you Leah."

"I don't want you to think that way. I want you to start believing that I'm a part of you and that you have me with you all the time. What you think you should be grateful to me for is actually to your own merit, Enzo," she looks at me with eyes that suddenly look sad.

"You're sad again," I worry.

"No, it's not sadness," she sighs. "These are different feelings, mixed feelings, but most of all, I'm proud. I feel pure and extraordinary pride," a tear falls and she wipes it away from her beautiful face. I approach her and kiss her passionately, and I don't stop. She kisses me back. We kiss and we hug. The passion begins to feel incredible. We don't stop, and we completely surrender to the moment that moves us toward something unknown.

"Enzo," she sighs, moving away from me.

"Enzo, I want to be careful, I don't want to hurt you. Enzo, I knew something had happened, I noticed you running away from passion and at the same time despising the act of making love, as if it were the greatest evil. For you, that act was not making love, but was just evil, an enormously great evil. I understand. I completely understand, and I know why my flirtation and the carefree way I went to bed with men, why it was so disgusting to you. I fully understand that now. Believe me; I don't want to hurt you. I watched how many times you were scared, and now it's clear to me. Enzo, I want you, I know you want me too, but I want you to want everything that happens to you, to happen to you, do you understand me?

I'm silent. She pulls up her chair at the other end of the terrace and drinks from her glass. I keep looking at her and say nothing. I try to develop my feelings and my opinion. I try to repeat her words and conclude what I think of them. I see her sitting on a chair, raising her legs and crouching like a small child, looking somewhere along the Arno River. She is beautiful, she is real, I know she is real and I really want her. I go through everything that can happen to me in my head, how to unroll a coil, how to unroll that coil that Leah told me I had to unroll- to start over. Everything that can happen to me is running through my head, and it's like watching a brand-new movie in front of me. I want to judge if I like it, and if I can watch it at all. A million scenes pass by me, a million small moments jump one after the other, and I just absorb them. They tickle my head gently, creating countless small images in front of my eyes. At one point, while all those little pictures live in my head playfully - I realise that I can and want to feel and experience it all for real. I realise that I want all this to happen to me and I'm ready for many new things. I also realise that this experience with Leah, from our acquaintance to this moment now, is like a long journey where you leave completely unprepared, without anything to bring, and you return completely changed, with absolutely everything you need.

You will never know exactly where you were, what exactly happened there, or for how long it was happening. You will only know that something changed forever after that trip and that you're no longer the same. Every time the image of Leah appears before my eyes, I know that I won't think of anything else but how her existence made me feel. The playfulness of my soul and the ability to fully feel it again will always be the greatest truth for me. Touching my heart with my hand and listening to it beat relentlessly, I will know that I have a reason to live, and I have something to tell. This time, my story will be untamed and incredibly cheerful, just like Leah.

It will happen spontaneously over time, leaving lasting traces of happiness and joy. Everyone's soul will be filled with hope and desire for a new beginning by hearing my story. Everyone's faces will be smiling, just like mine, as I tell them my truth.

Finally, I will always tell them to touch their hearts with their hands and hear their hearts beating relentlessly. It is the sound of strength, the sound of struggle, and the sound of victory. When we feel the playfulness of the soul from within, it simply means that someone has been there or may stay there forever, throwing us an unplanned party when all the ships seem to have sunk from the restless sea. Right in the heart of the storm, someone teaches us to swim, and shows us how to love all the waves.

Chapter 15

"Good afternoon, Doctor."

"Good afternoon, you've arrived."

"Yes. We're on time, aren't we?"

"Yes, yes. Let's go to my office, please. Sit down please. Would you like some coffee to drink?"

"I'd like some coffee please."

"Great, and for you, Mr. Moretti?"

"Coffee for me too, please. It may sound ridiculous, but after so much coffee in this hospital, I began to miss it. I often tell my friends that the best coffee I ever had, was here. I don't know if it's funny, but it is to me."

"I'll ask the nurse to bring it."

"Thank you, Doctor."

"Nurse, please, can you bring us three cappuccinos. Yes, three. Thank you."

"How's work, Doctor?"

"Same as always, Mrs. Moretti. We have a lot of work, and we try to finish it and progress as much as we can, I'm sure I don't have to tell you how it is."

"No, no; of course not."

"My wife knows this hospital by heart, Doctor. She knows every corner of it."

"Yes, I know every corner, because I cried in each of them."

"It's ok to cry when you're struggling dear. I am a man myself, but I cry when I need to."

"I understand Mr. and Mrs. Moretti. Now tell me, how is Enzo?

"Enzo ..."

"Come in, Nurse, come in. Leave the coffee here on the table. Thank you. Close the door, please. Thank you."

"How nice the coffee smells, that's why it's my favourite!"

"I'm glad."

"Thank you Doctor."

"Let's return to the subject, Mr. and Mrs.

Moretti. Tell me, how is Enzo's life going now that he's at home? What does he do, how does he behave, how is he with you? You know, although he regularly comes here to talk and check in with me, I always like to examine the situation a little deeper."

"Enzo is good. As you know, since he's been home, we visit you regularly and make sure he takes his medicine daily. He is calm, we observe it. We can see it. Everything is under control."

"Yes, but Mrs. Moretti, as I have explained to you many times before, his condition is very complex; being in control isn't enough to understand how he feels. I want to encourage you to get closer to him and get to know your son a little better."

"Doctor, we know our son very well. He is our son, that goes without saying."

"Okay, Mr. Moretti, but believe me, it is always possible to get to know him better. His condition complicates his character, and to be able to truly get to know him deeply, requires patience, desire, and time."

"We understand, Doctor. What do you suggest?"

"I don't suggest anything, Mrs. Moretti. I just encourage you. I encourage you to make mistakes. I encourage you to try. I encourage you to research and to find the right way to communicate with him."

"I'm so confused."

"Sir, I don't want to confuse you. Enzo hides in a world of his own, which we can only guess from the outside. His improvement is mostly due to the existence of that world, and the influence that that world has on his soul. When I said that this is his fight, I meant exactly that, but let's not stop there. I want you to try something new, I want you to delve a little deeper into Enzo's life and see things from a different angle. Enzo is a wonderful creature but he's not simple at all. Talk to him, ask him questions that really interest him, listen to what he has to say, learn from him, let him tell you, let him receive you into his world and be happy that your son is so special."

"You're right. Doctor, I don't know what we've been doing for so long. We just think we're seeing, when in fact we are blind. We became ignorant, we turned into machines. We have no patience, we have no understanding, and we have no empathy. So what if we love him, when we have no empathy for what is happening to him? We are guilty, doctor, guilty!"

"Calm down, ma'am. Please don't cry. It's

quite natural. Some things take a while to understand. Don't blame yourself for what you couldn't have known."

"No, Doctor, this isn't the case. It doesn't matter if we understand or not. Empathy has nothing to do with it. Empathy means support, interest, and compassion. We didn't have that. We made assumptions when all we had to do was to be there for him. Doctor, he told me everything. I understand now."

"I don't understand anything she is saying Doctor. Don't cry dear, come, calm down,"

"Let her talk, only then she will calm down. Mrs. Moretti, can you explain. What did Enzo tell you?"

"I can't calm down, I can't."

"Breathe. Just breathe. You have to tell me, this, it's important."

"You know, after he got home, he started painting again."

"I know. He talked about it when we decided to release him. He kept saying he couldn't wait to paint his beautiful world."

"Yes. At home he doesn't stop painting. He's not in a hurry, he paints slowly, but he enjoys it. Every day he draws a new line and he's happy. At times I even think he doesn't want to finish it.

I'll ask him what he's painting, and he'll answer, "I paint my world." The same answer every time. The other day I went into his room to take him his medicine and to see him, but when I entered, he was dressed in his father's suit. He looked great, as if it were his. The room smelled of women's perfume. I immediately recognised it as one of my perfumes. I couldn't understand what was happening. He was so well-groomed, standing in front of his easel and painting. When he saw me coming in, he smiled at me and kept working. I looked at the easel and saw his picture. He had painted a girl with long hair and a beautiful face. I didn't recognise her. I didn't know who she was. I didn't want to ask him about other things, I asked him what he was painting, and again, without hesitation, he said he was painting his world. I didn't know what to say. I left the medicine on the small table in his room, and as I left, I noticed a pair of women's shoes there. After looking at it carefully, I remembered it was mine. Why did he have them? I completely forgot that I had them at all.

I couldn't understand how Enzo found my shoes, and why he put them on the table in his room. I looked at him, and he didn't even notice me looking at him, he was completely engrossed in his painting. So I asked him.

"Enzo, son, why are those shoes here?" but he didn't answer. He just continued painting.

"Enzo, will you answer me?! Why are these shoes here?" I repeated, in a slightly anxious voice. Again, he didn't answer.

"I don't understand," I said aloud, sighing, and I bowed my head.

"You have to learn to believe in what you don't understand, Mom," he said, looking at me with a look I hadn't seen in his eyes for a long time. He smiled at me, looking like a handsome gentleman, dressed in a suit, standing proudly in front of his work of art. I saw my son, my Enzo, my child all grown up, my child with the purest soul and the warmest heart. I smiled at him too.

"Faith is created by the truth," he said, "and the truth is created by us."

The End

Acknowledgements

I want to thank my family for the biggest support. I want to thank my husband for staying with me through the most difficult times.

I want to thank Kingsley Publishers for giving me a chance to spread my wings internationally. I am eternally grateful.

Author Bio

Ksenija Nikolova is a Macedonian fiction author, and she has been writing since she was little. Her books abound with emotions, where characters' internal lives and battles are deeply described. She uses her voice in her books to raise mental health awareness and to diminish discrimination and narrow thinking.

She is the author of six books, and "All men love Leah" is her first book translated and published into English. She says she wrote this book in her darkest moments, but it was also this book which brought great light to her life.

Author Social Media

Facebook: Ksenija Nikolova
Instagram: @ksenijanikolova
Twitter: @Ksenijawrites

9 780620 947480